MR.
FAMOUS

MR. FAMOUS

carol wolper

RIVERHEAD BOOKS

a member of Penguin Group (USA) Inc.

New York · 2004

RIVERHEAD BOOKS
a member of
Penguin Group (USA) Inc.
375 Hudson Street
New York, NY 10014

Library of Congress Cataloging-in-Publication Data

Wolper, Carol, date.
  Mr. Famous / Carol Wolper.
    p.   cm.
  ISBN 1-57322-272-0
    1. Motion picture actors and actresses—Fiction.   2. Self-actualization
(Psychology)—Fiction.   3. Celebrities—Fiction.   4. Actors—Fiction.
I. Title: Mister Famous.   II. Title.
PS3573.O5678M7   2004   2004041481
813'.54—dc22

Printed in the United States of America
10   9   8   7   6   5   4   3   2   1

This book is printed on acid-free paper. ♾

Book design by Stephanie Huntwork

MR.
FAMOUS

henever Mr. Famous was troubled about something, he'd send me to Orso to pick up a pizza. Thin crust. Crushed red peppers. Mozzarella cheese. Only in a crisis would he allow himself to eat wheat or dairy. I know a lot about Mr. F's eating habits. I was his chef. He'd hired me a year ago, right before he did *Last Standing*, because his agent told him that if he was going to play the part of someone who annihilated a team of Philippine terrorists, he needed to look good in a medium shot wearing a tight T-shirt and maharishi pants. Okay, he's forty-six and shouldn't be wearing clothes inspired by teenage skateboarders, but Mr. F didn't question the wardrobe choice. He did, however, demand money in the budget for a personal trainer and nutritionist.

Enter me. I wasn't a nutritionist but he liked the way I looked. Not in a sexual way. More like in a home decorating way, as if I went well with the green vase on the kitchen table. I also have this quality about me—nonthreatening—

which, when it comes to job-hunting in Hollywood, is as important as making a good pasta pomodoro.

It was a strange time for me. I'd recently changed careers and broken up with my boyfriend Matt, who, I have to say, gets the credit for inadvertently setting me on a new job path. Trying to be a TV writer in Hollywood was turning me into a boring cynic, which made me feel so guilty about becoming a tinsel town cliché—and not even one of the more glamorous clichés, like demanding diva or nymphomaniac starlet—that I started cooking fancy meals as some form of compensation. Poor Matt, he had to listen to me rant about "the system." "My agent says I can't pitch my ideas to the network unless I'm partnered up with an established writer-producer. But how am I supposed to do that? All those big guys have about a million of their own ideas and aren't looking to share credit or cash." Matt felt no need to answer and in fact tuned me out. The surest way to get him to tune back in was to whip up a bowl of tagliolini with prawns and radicchio.

To my great surprise, I found that I was better at creating recipes than I was at creating sitcoms. Eventually, though, it occurred to me that Matt loved my lobster ravioli more than he loved me. Or maybe he was just too busy loving himself. High maintenance doesn't begin to describe him. Here's Matt in an arrogant and needy mood—an especially exhausting combination. A few months before we split up, he informed me we'd be having dinner with one of his prospective business partners. Matt was trying to put together the financing for a small restaurant/bar that he hoped would attract the young Hollywood crowd. As I was getting ready, he came into the bedroom to tell me that it was his dinner, his meeting, and I shouldn't talk.

"At all?" I asked, incredulous.

"You know what I mean," he replied. "Don't take over the conversation."

Okay, let me just say this right out. I'm smarter than my ex-boyfriend and we both know it. And because I'm smart, I understood that playing the bimbo for one dinner could be a gesture of love and grace—as well as, possibly, an interesting exercise in self-restraint. So I went along with his program until halfway through the meal. That's when he started kicking me under the table to save the evening, which had deteriorated into a discussion of whether ESPN was on channel 26 or 27.

That's what I get for dating a paranoid narcissist. What was I thinking? He also hated the fact that I had begun to work for Mr. Famous, a nickname I'd come up with out of affection, but Matt made it sound like a slur. He resented my boss because Matt had once tried to be an actor and never got past a brief part on a soap. His résumé was only one step up from Joey Tribbiani's.

Pizza night was becoming a habit ever since January 12, the date of the Claire Neville incident. Classy name. Classy family. Trashy girl. Claire grew up in the wealthiest neighborhood in one of the wealthiest towns in Connecticut. Her grandfather's name was on a building at Yale. Her father's name was on the wing of a hospital. But Claire was whacked. She was one of those rich girls who gets away with being crazy long after the usual expiration date. But one day even these girls pass the point where outlandish is cute. In this case, that point hit last summer, around Claire's thirty-third birthday.

It was right around then that she was featured in a magazine article about East Coast socialites who had relocated to Hollywood. The other three women in the article posed, dressed in some version of California casual. Claire chose to be shot in the doorway of her walk-in closet wearing nothing but her La Perla underwear. At the time she justified it by saying she was a jewelry designer and the exposure was good for her career. A month after the magazine hit the newsstands, Claire dropped her jewelry line and took up photography, specializing in self-portraits. She recently had a show at a gallery on Las Palmas—twenty blow-up shots of herself naked.

Those acts of self-obsession and self-promotion set the stage for what became "the Claire Incident." First, I'll give you the version that ran in the press. It made news because as whacked as Claire is, she's a *name*. And when a *name* is drunk and gets into an accident, THAT makes the papers. And when that accident involves a car going off the top of Mulholland, in some Hollywood version of Princess Grace's last drive to Monaco, THAT inspires a headline. And when the car crashes onto property owned by a former studio executive, who that night just happened to be having a dinner for a former U.S. president, THAT warrants a spot on the front page. And when the *name* gets out of the crumpled car, drunk, with a bleeding cut on her arm and a smile, THAT brings out the TV cameras. And when it's discovered that there's a gun in the glove compartment which was recently fired, THAT gets phones ringing all over Hollywood. And when the intoxicated *name* tells the cops that she was just getting in a little shooting practice earlier in the day and laughs, THAT results in a flurry of e-mails. And when the *name* blabs to the press that she just had a fight with her boyfriend and slugged him so hard she's sure he'll wake up with a black eye, THAT makes the World Wide Web in about two seconds. And when the *name* looks right into the camera and says, "Isn't that something, seeing as my boyfriend is a big action-hero movie star and I only weigh a hundred and ten pounds," well, THAT guarantees that papers, TV, the Internet, voice mail, faxes, e-mails, pagers and Blackberrys will be trading rumors for days.

There is another version. Mr. F claims that Claire could go from fun to nightmare faster than any girl he's ever known. He said that on that particular day, she started off being Claire at her best. But as they were driving back to the house after dinner, she asked him if they'd be going to Paris in May for the French Open. He said he couldn't plan that far in advance. Apparently, she took that to mean not only wouldn't he commit to a vacation, he would never, ever commit to her.

Mr. F said she went berserk. His description of her behavior made it sound like things rapidly escalated into a scene that sounds like Ibsen as interpreted by Quentin Tarantino. Picture Nora's righteousness with Jackie Brown's taste for revenge.

. . .

We were on the fourteenth pizza since the night of the incident. In real time that was a month. Every other day a trip to Orso, and the rest of the time, sashimi, to make up for the calories consumed the night before. Schizo eating habits were common in L.A. Back in the eighties, the tofu/cocaine diet was a favorite. And the most astonishing thing was that no one found this astonishing.

I made up a salad to go along with the fourteenth pizza in order to justify my existence as a chef, and because I couldn't handle feeling like a glorified delivery girl. I brought it outside to where Mr. F was sitting in a lounge chair by the pool. I set it down on a small table next to Mr. Famous's tortoiseshell-framed sunglasses. It was late afternoon and the sun had just, minutes before, sunk below the canyon. A torn envelope was on the ground next to him. In his hands he held a piece of paper, which he stared at, shell-shocked, as if he'd just read his own obituary. He groaned as I approached.

"Do you fucking believe this, Lucy? [My name is Lucinda but Mr. F preferred my nickname.] Do you fucking believe this?"

He handed what I now saw was a printed invitation to the *Vanity Fair* Oscar party.

"It's an invitation to Hollywood's version of the stockade," he said.

"It is?" I wasn't getting it. I knew Mr. F went to the same event last year because I saw a photo of him in *People.*

"What time is the invitation for?" He asked as if he

were teaching remedial reading. I took another look at the invitation. "Eleven-thirty."

"That's right. Eleven-thirty. And what time was I invited for last year?"

I had no idea. It's not like I was his date. He just assumed the details of his public life were national headlines.

"Nine?" I guessed.

"*Nine?*" He looked at me as if I'd gotten my own name wrong. "*Five.* Five o'clock. The A-list invitation. For the sit-down dinner."

"Oh, that's right," I said. A willingness to appear stupid was sometimes part of this job, not too different from what I'd had to do in my last relationship. It was a pattern I kept repeating. I made a mental note to look into that.

"You see what that nutcase has done to my life?" He sounded less angry than tired.

Claire was now only referred to as "nutcase" or sometimes "that nutcase."

"I thought *Vanity Fair* liked a few scandals at their party," I said.

"They do. But apparently they've already filled their infamy quota. I'm falling between the cracks here."

I sat on an adjoining lounge chair. "Why do you care about some party?"

He didn't answer. And I didn't push. For a few minutes everything got very quiet. Everything. In this private enclave of houses that looked like hotels, the nearest neighbor could be seen but usually not heard. Still, the silence I'm talking about was exceptional. No sound of a dog barking or even a car winding its way somewhere through the canyons. Quiet was one of the luxuries that came with this expensive address, but occasionally it could make you feel as if you were cut off from the rest of the world. Not a good thing for most Hollywood people, who, regardless of their success, feared being cut off from the action. Most people up here liked turning off their phones only when they knew the calls were still rolling in. It was my belief that people who were good at being alone had a better chance of surviving in Hollywood. I made a mental note to beef up on my loner skills.

I watched with concern as Mr. Famous got up and walked over to the pool. He was wearing jeans, a black T-shirt and no shoes. He teetered on the edge.

"I can't even swim anymore," he said as he looked straight down into the water. I couldn't tell if that meant he was physically incapable or had just lost all desire to do something that was good for him. At that moment he reminded me of a character in a Ross Macdonald mystery novel. One of those guys who had taken the Southern California dream as far as he could and then had taken his nightmares further. I noticed his hands were trembling slightly. He stuck the left one, the one closest to me, in his pocket. "In my last movie I leaped off a cliff into raging waters without a moment's hesitation."

I didn't dispute this, though the truth was, a stunt double did the dive. But the difference didn't matter to him and it certainly didn't matter to his fans.

"You've got to help me," he said.

"Of course I'll help you," I replied. "Whatever you need. It'll all be okay." I had no idea what I was promising, but I sincerely wanted to live up to whatever offer I'd just made. Not because I thought I was specially chosen. I know that famous people often turn to whoever's around at the moment and give that person the job of fixing things. It's a question of timing, not talent.

"Okay then," he said, without ever turning in my direction. I was happy to avoid eye contact while he was in this vulnerable state. Emotional intimacy was the edge I teetered on. And I wasn't about to put even a toe in that water.

A gush of wind picked up the *Vanity Fair* invitation and blew it into the pool, where it floated, facedown, like a corpse. I definitely had Ross Macdonald on the brain.

"So, what are you going to do?" Mr. F asked after giving me a few minutes to think about it. "How are you going to fix this?"

I scrambled to come up with an answer, or at least a plan. Never before had I been faced with the challenge of saving an action hero on the verge of an F. Scott Fitzgerald–style "crack-up." I quickly formulated a mental list. There were a few people I could have called right then for advice or assistance: Lawrence, Mr. Famous's best friend; Isabel, his ex-wife; or Alex, his agent. But I suspected that getting to the heart of this matter was a big job. Bigger than me. Bigger than Mr. F's inner circle. Only one thing to do. I called Dr. Davenport.

two

C laire didn't have a line on her face but she looked old. It was the side angle that betrayed her. She was sitting on the couch talking earnestly on the phone to a girlfriend. The light from the window revealed her most unflattering angle. There was a bit of extra skin under the neck and slight folds along the jawline that in another ten years, without surgery, would turn into baby jowls. Mr. Famous kept these thoughts to himself, though he found them unsettling.

It was around three in the afternoon and the two of them had had a late lunch and were now lazing around, killing time until their eight P.M. dinner reservation at The Ivy. They were going to hook up with Lawrence and his date, Rikki, an aspiring actress who paid her bills by teaching spinning classes twice a day, five days a week. With the exception of professional athletes, Claire had always had a problem with girls who spent an inordinate amount of time exercising. How could she not have disdain for someone whose idea of reading is scanning *People* magazine while on the treadmill. What is it with men who have great taste in everything except the girls they date? Once, she'd even posed that question directly to Lawrence, who was quick with an answer. "Too much class in a man is boring. And it requires too much vanity, which is not an attractive quality." She thought about that for a while and, though not entirely sure what Lawrence meant, had since incorporated it into her repertoire of witticisms.

As she laughed at something, Claire raised her head and shifted her position. In doing so, she removed all traces of aging and any Connecticut reserve and was back to being the perky thirty-three-year-old who could pass for twenty-eight and act like she was still twenty-two. Especially when she was giggling on the phone with a girlfriend. Claire's youthful spirit was a big part of what made her so desirable to Mr. Famous. "She's got a sparkle to her" is how he'd once described her to Lawrence.

"Got to watch out for sparkle," Lawrence replied somberly.

"Why?"

"Very small step from sparkle to out of her fucking mind."

Mr. F sifted through a stack of paperwork his assistant had left for him. Mostly checks to be signed, a few memos and one contract for the option Mr. F wanted to renew. It would be his sixth two-year renewal for the book *Skate*, which had absolutely nothing to do with skating. The novella, written by a man from Michigan, was a fable about a factory worker whose life was pretty grim but he always found something to be happy about. Unfortunately, his good mood got on the nerves of the people he worked with and they conspired to give him a reason to be sad. There was a lot more to the story and it wasn't precious. It was sexy and gritty and sporadically violent. And frequently very, very funny.

It had been Mr. F's brother Ned's favorite book. Dead Ned. He'd died twenty-two years earlier, when he was only twenty-four. Pneumonia was the reason on the death certificate but the real cause was a genetic degenerative muscular disease. Mr. F had been thinking about Ned a lot lately, as he did every January, which was the month Ned died. He remembered the day his brother had given him *Skate,* along with a few other books. Ned did a lot of reading from the bed he almost never left—unless it was to go to the hospital. And yet he never seemed depressed. Whatever troubles or dark moods he had to deal with were never downloaded onto anyone else. More impressive, he was always excited about some new story or idea. "Mini epiphanies," he called them. His curiosity and enthusiasm never waned. How did he do that? Mr. F wondered. How is that even fucking possible? Could clarity and perspective be the upside of knowing you're probably not going to live long? Big price to pay for the ability to "be here now," Mr. F concluded. Big fucking price.

Claire's hand slipped inside the neckline of Mr. F's T-shirt. She knew exactly which spot held all his tension and began to massage it away. Of course just when he relaxed into it, she stopped. Picking up the contract, she studied the first page. "You're renewing?"

"Yeah. Have to. Can't let it go."

"Are you ever going to even try to get this made?"

"It's not that simple. This is the kind of thing I could probably only get financing for if the budget isn't too big and I'd just made the studio a fortune with back-to-back blockbusters."

She moved to the front of the chair where he was sitting and worked a knee between his legs. She also knew the exact spot that would get his dick going. She flipped to page two of the contract. Talk about multitasking.

"Where did I read that when Irving Thalberg ran the studio he made a point of doing at least one quality film a year, even though he knew it wouldn't earn a profit. He considered it a public service. No, wait, I didn't read that. I heard it. It was in that film *The Last Tycoon*. Bob De Niro says that line."

She always felt a tinge of self-consciousness calling him Bob. It's not as if she'd ever met him. But Mr. F, who did one movie with him eight years before, called him Bob, and after a couple of conversations where she'd say Robert and he'd say Bob, she'd adopted Mr. F's lingo. If pressed on the issue she'd say it made communication easier but it was also true that she figured it was one of the privileges that came with being a movie star's girlfriend. If she was going to name-drop, she was going to name-drop nicknames.

She placed the *Skate* contract back down on the coffee table. "I always loved the title."

He took her hand and put it on his dick. "What else do you love?"

She beamed a full-on "I am totally delighted with the direction this is going in" kind of smile.

"If I tell you, can I have it?" she said as she began to unzip. It wasn't just another provocative line, the kind that's usually delivered by Hollywood girls who have been taught at an early age how to get a guy off. Mr. F had had his share of girls who knew how to act sexy but not a clue as to how to be sexy. Claire was different, he'd concluded. That sparkle in her eyes suggested she'd never settle for a fake orgasm. And if she did fake one, she was the best faker he'd ever met.

three

want to find the person who said there's no such thing as bad publicity and tell them they're the anti-Christ and that they've created a breed of malignant narcissists. That thought occurred to me as I was in the produce section of Bristol Farms, an upscale market with the de rigueur touches: coffee bar, sushi bar and top-of-the-line takeout. Lots of those around L.A., but this place surpassed the competition with its grilled panini. Yes, you can get your Santa Fe turkey, cheese and pepper sandwich made hot to go. It's also one of the few stores that carries Domaine Ott, a wine my friend Elizabeth West turned me on to—which is alternately known as the wicked rosé or liquid ecstasy.

was shopping for artichokes when I looked up to find a classic malignant narcissist at the end of the aisle. Claire. She had her compact out and was checking her makeup under one of the dimmed overhead lights. That was another plus about Bristol Farms. As part of their political correctness, they kept the wattage down to conserve energy. Or at least that was what someone told me. However, I suspected it was also because they understood that most of their customers were women who would gladly drive out of their way and pay extra to shop under flattering lighting. That was a bigger draw than a grilled panini or even a bottle of dangerous rosé.

Claire spotted me before I had a chance to dart. She sashayed over and kissed me on the cheek, narrowly missing a poke in the eye from the artichoke in my hand.

"Always loved the way you do artichokes," she said, taking a step back. "What is that sauce you serve them with?"

"Mayonnaise."

"Really? Maybe I'm confusing your artichokes with someone else's." She laughed and gripped my arm as if the joke was at some third person's expense instead of mine.

I glanced into her shopping basket, which she carried in the crux of her arm as if it were a stylish tote. Tampax. Vodka. Lots of lemons. Club soda. Nouriche yogurt drink. And one box of frozen quesadillas. Sticking up between the groceries were three copies of *Daily Variety.*

"Why three?" I asked.

"Because I'm in it." She pulled a copy out and turned to the party page. It was a picture of her at a premiere, sitting at a table with one of the movie's actors and his manager.

"That shot cracks me up," she said. "Doesn't it look like I'm leaning over to do a line of blow? But I was just searching in my bag for a mirror. I'm obsessing over this mascara I've been using. Can't figure out why it keeps flaking and I end up with goo in the corner of my eyes." Then, as if bored with her own obsession, she took back the *Variety* and checked out the contents of my shopping cart. "Well, aren't you healthy? Bee pollen. Carrots. Come on, throw in some salsa and chips. Victor will love it. Of course, later, after the bag is empty, he'll blame you for bringing it into the house."

Victor was Mr. F's real name. A perfectly lovely name, but there was something about the way Claire said it, with that clipped boarding school accent of hers, that made it seem more appropriate for a stuffy royal than an All-American action hero.

"You know we haven't spoken in a while," she said, almost wistfully. "I was thinking of calling him."

"Well, you know the number," I replied, trying to remain as neutral as possible.

"Is he seeing anyone?"

No way was I going to answer that. "He's doing fine." The non-answer answer was becoming my specialty. Not that I'd signed a confidentiality agreement, but respecting Mr. F's privacy was part of the job.

"I get it. Can't talk about your boss. That's fine." She touched my arm as if excusing me for being discreet.

"And he is my friend," I added.

She let out a short, sharp laugh. "He's your friend until he doesn't need you anymore. That's how famous people operate."

"Not just famous people," I said.

"But the transition is shorter with the famous. Here today, forgotten tomorrow." She patted my arm again. "Not just gone. Forgotten."

· · ·

As I finished up my shopping, I kept coming back to what she had said and how she'd zeroed in on the one thing Mr. F lacked and she had in spades. I had seen Mr. F go from being "brothers" with some guy to barely returning his phone calls, and when he did, never spending more than the minute or two it took to politely claim to be too busy to get together. Granted this was a way of life in Hollywood, but it always made me feel slightly woozy, reminding me of just how unstable the ground is out here. Claire, on the other hand, kept in touch with anyone who would keep in touch with her. It may take her a while to call back, but once you're her friend, you're always on the list. I think it was her version of being a snob. She was so blueblood she didn't have to limit her friends to those she needed. Doesn't mean she didn't have a whole other set of needs that ran her life.

While I was putting the groceries in my car, I spotted Claire behind the wheel of her Jaguar. As she headed out of the parking lot, a guy in a Jeep Cherokee leaned on his horn and swerved to avoid a collision. I doubt Claire was even aware of the near miss seeing as her CD player was blasting Dido, which no doubt added to her wistfulness. She had her cell phone to her ear, and when the call went through, she lowered the volume of the music. I got a glimpse of her animated face as she chatted with whoever was on the other end. My gut told me she was calling Mr. F. Claire may be a snob but she was a snob who hated to be forgotten.

four

I made a salad for lunch. Grilled ahi tuna, lettuce, tomatoes, light on the dressing. Alex, Mr. F's agent, was sitting at the kitchen table, with only me for company. Mr. F was on his way back from his first session with Dr. Davenport and was running late. He'd already called twice from the car. First to complain about the traffic and then to kill time while he was stuck in the gridlock. Alex's anxiety was cranked up a notch by the delay. He had a meeting back at his office at three P.M. and he was starving. He was also a regular visitor at the house so it wasn't a stretch for him to take me up on the invitation to sit down and have a bite. Mr. F wouldn't mind. In fact, I knew he'd probably prefer it because Alex was one of those guys who chowed down in five minutes and expected you to do the same. Long, three-course business dinners were torture for him. He was the ultimate cut-to-the-chase guy. Eat because you had to but don't make a big deal about it. Get to the point of the meeting. Figure it out. Wrap it up fast. And, at a restaurant, always tip the valet ahead of time so your car will be waiting when you exit. Relaxation wasn't in his vocabulary. Was his wife okay with that? Did he drive his kids crazy? If his impatience didn't, then his habit of asking blunt, personal questions might. In between bites of his lunch, he fired a few inquiries in my direction.

"So you got a boyfriend these days?" He wasn't being flirtatious. Alex wouldn't waste valuable time on an affair when that time could be spent making money.

"We broke up."

"Was that the kid I saw you having breakfast with at Barney's?" Alex referred to anyone younger than himself as a kid.

"No, that's Lou. We see each other occasionally but it's not a relationship."

"What does Lou do?"

"Whatever he wants." It wasn't true but I wasn't in the mood to divulge Lou's bio or any further information about my sex life.

"Then he must be young and rich. Or a psychopath."

"None of the above."

I refilled my glass of iced tea as Alex worked diligently on his salad. The questions stopped. Guess he figured there was nothing I could tell him that he needed to know. To him I was probably just another girl who had grown up in Southern California and had ended up in L.A. looking for action. That would only be of interest to him if I'd *found* action in the entertainment business and could be an element in some deal he was putting together. I was a non-element in an element-chasing market, which meant all I merited, at most, was a passing curiosity.

We sat there in silence, except for the sound of Alex

chewing. Though only in his early forties, he seemed much older. He struck me as the kind of person who went from childhood to middle age without ever stopping at adolescence. Hard to imagine him wearing Levi's and a T-shirt. Impossible to imagine him with a joint in his mouth. He'd have no use for anything that might slow him down, mellow him out. He was the spiritual offspring of Sammy Glick, except with less flamboyance and a better education.

Fifteen minutes after sitting down to lunch, Alex checked his watch and then pushed his empty plate aside. He got up and went over to the window, stood there for a moment looking out toward the backyard, where Lauren, Mr. F's fourteen-year-old daughter, and her best friend, Ceci, were hanging out by the pool.

"Who are they?" he asked.

"That's Lauren and a friend of hers from school."

"That's Lauren? When did she turn into Britney Spears?"

"She's almost fifteen. And I'd say about six months ago."

"She's living here now?"

"Just visiting for the day. Her mother gets back from New York tonight."

I didn't mind answering those questions because it was all harmless. Yes, Lauren was growing up fast. Yes, she spent time with her father. Yes, her mother, Isabel, liked to travel, preferably on someone's private plane. In fact, Isabel left Mr. F years ago for a restaurant-chain king who had his own jet. Not that Mr. F minded. From what I heard, he was juggling a couple of actresses at the time. And when the restaurant king moved on, Isabel moved on to a Warner Brothers exec with access to his company's G4. She was a jet slut, but she claimed she came by it honestly. Commercial travel triggered her claustrophobia. Yeah, right. It triggered mine, too, but I wasn't blowing anyone for a free ride. I simply stayed on the ground. Not a great solution, but nothing would make me more claustrophobic than having an unwanted dick in my face.

Alex dwelled at the window a moment longer before turning away. "The things those girls will be offered," he said, shaking his head. I couldn't tell if he had a fatherly concern for them or was thinking ahead to what ten percent of those offerings might bring.

A half hour later, Mr. F showed up. I'd become expert at reading all signs to determine his mood, partly because as an employee who worked in my boss's house, it was in my best interest to gauge his shifting temperament. It was also because I had the standard fascination that comes with being a spectator in a movie star's world. I found myself unobtrusively studying Mr. F, trying to figure out if celebrities are different because they're famous, or famous because they're different. Talent and looks aside, I wondered if Mr. F also possessed some other quality that assured him of life on a bigger stage. Plus, the fact that for months I'd been working my way through the entire collection of Ross Macdonald's detective novels brought out the amateur sleuth in me.

When my boss chose to park right out front, not in the garage, that told me the meeting with Alex was important. The sound of his car door slamming shut told me that whatever relief he may have gotten from his session with Davenport had been wiped out by the traffic on the 405. Easy stuff to figure out. A ten-year-old could do it. But I was proud of myself for being able to read him based on his keys. Mr. F had certain habits that he maintained religiously. He always put his keys on the kitchen counter, always to the right of the countertop TV. Always. Unless he was really excited about something and then he'd walk in and just drop them on the kitchen table. But if he was in a bad mood or anxious about something, he left them in the ignition. When he walked into the kitchen keyless, I knew he wasn't a happy guy and there was a good chance we were in store for Mr. F as Steve Verne, the character he played in his first hit action flick. It was a character he often turned to when he needed a buffer between himself and whatever was stressing him out. He took the Steve part seriously, as if the name and the role gave him license to tap into McQueen's cool quotient. "Hey," he said nonchalantly, as if he hadn't run three red lights to get here sooner and Alex hadn't been waiting for forty-five minutes.

"Next time you're coming to my side of town." Alex sounded serious, though no one in Hollywood would take that remark seriously. Mr. F may be slipping when it came to *Vanity Fair*'s party list but he still had some juice at the box office. And movie stars don't trudge down to their agents' offices for a meeting. All meetings (and all girls) come to them. Rules of the game.

"Why not?" Mr. F replied, as if driving all the way down to the flats of Beverly Hills in the middle of the day to a building that had no valet (Mr. F hated underground parking) was a quirky but interesting adventure. Doesn't matter what he said, the three of us knew that would never happen.

I placed Mr. F's lunch on the table and put a cappuccino down in front of Alex. He scraped off the foamy milk. "Not into this girlie stuff," he said as if he were tearing off lace that I'd stupidly put around the collar of one of his black cashmere crewnecks. Meanwhile, Mr. F examined his plate of leafy greens. He sifted through the arugula, the baby cherry tomatoes, the pine nuts.

"Fancy," he said as if his usual was chopped iceberg and Kraft bottled dressing. It was the Steve in him talking. Blue-collar Steve who lived on coffee shop food and didn't care because he was too busy being a tough detective working the crime-filled streets of San Francisco.

"Yeah, I like to get fancy occasionally." I smiled. I could go with it. I could play my part. I could improvise, ad-lib and, if need be, lie. We're all actors here in L.A. whether we do it professionally or not. It's something you pick up as easily as a suntan.

left them alone to talk. At first I took my own cup of cappuccino, with lots and lots of girlie foam on it, outside to the patio. The L.A. *Times* was on the table as well as a few magazines Lauren had brought over. *Elle. Glamour. Jane. InStyle.* I flipped through their pages. When you know the real deal, it's hard to read some of this stuff. I perused an article on a TV actress photographed in the garden of her Hollywood Hills home. She talked about growing roses and hanging out with her dog Sam. Okay, the girl's a coke whore. Doesn't mean coke whores can't love their dogs and their flowers, but this article put so much gel on the lens, it might as well have been a Madonna video. Why aren't these magazine editors at least a little judgmental? By the way, I don't get people who say, "So-and-so is so judgmental," as if it's unfair. Of course, sometimes it is, but at least it's an opinion.

I continued to read these magazines because they were so useful at distracting me from my growing anxiety about Mr. F. However, not even an article on the perfect home-made facial scrub using fruits and vegetables could shut out the audible debate coming from the kitchen. Mr. F was still using his Steve voice, which is usually too cool to get loud. This time, uncharacteristically, it was upped a few decibels after Alex informed him that the test screening of his upcoming movie, *Last Standing*, had not gone well.

"You advised me to do that piece of shit," Mr. F screamed, but I knew he was just venting. He'd been excited about the project, calling it "a different kind of action film."

Alex retained his even tone even though he, too, got louder. "Victor, just 'cause you sell your soul doesn't mean you get what you want. There are no guarantees here. You can sell yourself and end up with nothing. Selling your soul is not an insurance policy—it's a lottery ticket." He took a moment to catch his breath. "Not that I'm saying you sold your soul. I'm just reminding you that this business is a game of gambles, guesses, luck and moving on."

"Then what am I paying you for?"

"Because I'm the best at what I do."

"Well, maybe the best isn't the issue. Maybe I need to try my luck at another casino."

I didn't stay to hear the rest. I didn't want to witness a Hollywood quarrel between a declining star and his agent. It was a little too Sunset Boulevard for me. I picked up my coffee cup and the Calendar and Food sections of the *Times*, figuring I'd take them down to the sitting area on the other side of the tennis court. It was my favorite part of the property. A beautifully carved stone bench was set in front of a large outdoor fireplace. It was Isabel's contribution. Apparently, during her marriage to Mr. Famous, she'd haul their dinner guests down there for cocktail hour. The staff would set up a makeshift bar and martinis would be served. It was all very elegant at twilight, and very peaceful during the day. I had to pass by the pool area to get to this piece of canyon paradise. As I did, Lauren called me over. She and Ceci were drinking diet Cokes, though neither weighed over 100 pounds. They were flipping through *Teen People* and *Cosmo Girl*.

"Who would you rather be?" Lauren asked. "J.Lo or Gwyneth?"

I didn't answer right away, mostly because it wasn't a question I could relate to.

"See, it's not easy," said Ceci. "But I say J.Lo."

Lauren made a face, as if to say you've got to be kidding. "She can't sing."

"Neither can Gwyneth," Ceci countered.

"But Gwyneth isn't trying to be a rock star."

They both looked at me to decide the issue. I glanced down at *Cosmo Girl*, which happened to be opened to a Guess advertisement. "I'd rather be her," I said, pointing to the girl in the ad, who was dressed in low-waisted lace-up jeans, a tiny top and a jacket. It wasn't her casual but sexy clothes and fabulous turquoise jewelry that caught my attention as much as her attitude. Her big, wild hair. Her carefree manner. And most of all, the expression of contentment on her face, which looked like it had everything to do with the hunky guy who had his arm around her and inside the waist of those low-rise pants. The girl looked like she was having a lot more fun than Gwyneth or J.Lo. And the fact that she was anonymous made her even more appealing. I ignored the likely possibility that the girl was a struggling model who only wished she could be a star. I preferred to see her simply as a lively girl with a hot boyfriend. She might be posing but she was no poseur. Or at least that was my fantasy.

"I'd definitely rather be her," I said.

"Who is she?" Ceci asked.

"She's no one," Lauren replied.

"She looks like she's having a pretty good time," I said.

Ceci took another glance. "She's not even smiling."

Lauren picked up the magazine and studied the page. "Okay, maybe," she conceded, giving me a point, or half a point, for my input.

Ceci looked baffled by this mini-alliance and looked to Lauren for an explanation.

"Think about it," Lauren said. "Do cover girls ever look like they're having a good time?"

"Not on the covers but sometimes inside. You know, one of those candid shots when they're at some event or something."

"Find one," Lauren said, tossing her the issue of *Cosmo Girl*.

I left the two of them looking for signs of real life in the pages of a glossy magazine. I knew they weren't going to find what they were looking for. But if I were just fifteen years old, I wouldn't want anyone telling me that.

An hour later, when I got back up to the house, Alex was gone. Mr. F was back to being himself. "Steve" had left the building but my boss was not alone. Dr. Ping, his acupuncturist, was there to administer his weekly treatment. Mr. F was lying on the living room couch as Dr. Ping applied his needles. A dozen of them jutted out from Mr. F's face. Despite his claim that these needles had a medicinal purpose, I knew what I was witnessing was a New Age face-lift. The theory was that a twenty-minute treatment once a week eliminated (or at least prevented) facial sagging. Acupuncture. Facials. Laser treatments. Botox. Collagen. They were all part of the new male vanity. Though I prefer men who age naturally and even think that gravity makes them sexier, I understood that Mr. Famous wasn't yet ready to relinquish his role as an all-American heartthrob.

"That's some guy you sent me to," he said sarcastically the second I walked in. I noticed he had a half-eaten candy bar on the table next to him. I'd bought it because Lauren has a thing for frozen Snickers.

"You didn't like Dr. Davenport?"

"What was *that*?" he shouted. He wasn't talking to me but to Dr. Ping, who stuck the last needle in a spot near Mr. F's neck, apparently with a little more force than usual. I think it was punishment for that candy bar.

"Cancer prevention," the acupuncturist quietly reminded him before stepping outside to give us privacy. Or maybe he just wanted a break from having to deal with an aging actor on a sugar rush.

"You didn't like Dr. Davenport?" I repeated. I had no trouble pursuing the topic while Mr. F was lying there with needles stuck all over his face. I'd been in his employ long enough to know he didn't mind having the help see him mid-maintenance, and I'd gotten used to having a conversation with someone who looked a little like Pinhead from *Hellraiser III.*

"I love paying someone a hundred and fifty dollars so they can tell me that I've paid so much attention to my public persona that there's no real me left."

Mr. F was putting a stupid spin on Davenport's message, making it sound like some lame statement found in an introductory psych class. "What a gig that is," he continued. "You get people coming to your office and they've got to be on time or it's their dime. You get to sit there in your big leather chair and tell them what they're doing wrong, which doesn't mean you're right. And if they don't agree, they're the sick one."

I could have picked apart this summation but opted to simply point out that the glass was not totally empty. "But the good news is that they're always on time. You don't have to wait for them."

"I don't have to wait for anybody." He laughed mockingly, as if everything was now a joke.

I wondered if he knew that I'd heard about the poor test screening of his movie. I wondered if he knew that his face went into a grimace whenever reading about The Rock's latest movie.

"So I guess you won't be going back to the doctor?" I said. "Are you also off the diet?"

He finished off the candy bar. "I have a big appetite. I'm eating for two now. Me and my persona."

I nodded as if that made sense. I didn't point out that if Davenport was right, it was really just for one. I nodded again as if he'd spoken again. What could I say? That you can't just call up your real self and invite it back home. You dumped it. Why should it want to move back in? Your real self can't be seduced back with a few words. It's got its pride. It's not a bimbo who needs her rent paid. And even those girls hold out a little. I could easily picture Davenport delivering the bad news. "Get ready for a whole new definition of playing hard to get," he'd say. "Finding the self you threw away could be the hardest thing you've ever had to do."

Which would explain why Mr. F sat there quietly for a few moments before he abruptly got up (losing a few needles in the process), went upstairs to the master suite and didn't come down for three days.

five

You can never find a stamp when you need one." In one hand Mr. Famous held the envelope and signed contract for his option on the book *Skate*. With the other, he sifted through the contents in the top drawer of his bureau. He poked around for a few more seconds before giving up the search. He was standing in his bedroom, next to the window that overlooked grounds that had recently been re-landscaped for a pricey fifty thousand dollars. Claire had encouraged him to get rid of the "boring perennials" and to put in something wilder. She referred to the project as their first co-production.

"I thought I had some," Claire said as she dug through her Prada bag. She searched through her Bottega Veneta wallet. "Guess not." She tossed the wallet and bag on the floor. "I think I've got some in the car." She was sitting in one of the big comfy chairs that faced the TV, which was tuned to the local news. She picked up the remote and powered off.

Mr. F turned around. "I was watching that."

"No you weren't. We didn't come upstairs to get the weather report." She handed him the remote anyway. Her philosophy of relationships was based on the assumption that men need to think they're calling the shots. Mr. F took the remote, held on to it for a second before decisively tossing it aside.

It was a great afternoon fuck. Mr. F occasionally joked to his friends that though he and Claire may not be in love, their bodies were. And when the sex was over, Claire was not needy. Unlike every other woman he'd ever been with, she wasn't interested in hanging out in bed and cuddling. In that respect, and that respect only, she was like a guy. It occurred to him that she might be the perfect match for him. It might be time to have a real girlfriend, he thought. It could be nice to live with someone again, at least on weekends.

Claire got out of bed and pushed the covers around. "Where'd my underwear go?" She looked under the bed. "Won't do to have one of your other girlfriends find them." She was joking. Sex made her confident and at that moment she was unconcerned about any potential competition. Sex also made her manic.

She found her lacy thong, slipped it on and did a little dance step for her lover's amusement. She gathered up her clothes and kept up the erotic performance while getting dressed. It was a kind of striptease in reverse. When she was fully clothed, she picked up her bag, keys and his unstamped envelope.

"I'll mail it for you, sweetie," she said and then gave him the kind of kiss that could inspire another hour of playtime.

"Thanks, love."

"What time are you going to pick me up?"

"Reservation is at eight, so how about eight?"

A frown fleetingly crossed Claire's face. That meant they'd be at least fifteen minutes late, maybe twenty. She considered it rude to keep friends waiting at a restaurant but it wasn't her job to teach Mr. F manners. Not just now anyway.

"Whatever you want." She smiled.

After she left, he turned the TV back on, flipping through the channels until he happened to come upon a movie on HBO. The actress on the screen was someone he'd had a brief affair with four years ago. He noted that she looked good. Better than he'd remembered. On second thought, maybe he wasn't ready for a live-in girlfriend. Not yet.

six

There was a time, maybe twenty years earlier, when Mr. Famous was often compared to Michael Hutchence. Like the lead singer from the eighties band INXS, he had the same dark good looks, the same reputation for wild partying and an unbridled energy that jumped off the screen. No surprise they'd even slept with some of the same women. Back then, Mr. F wasn't married to Isabel. That didn't happen till Lauren was five, and marriage and fatherhood hardly slowed him down.

I mention this because I should have had some empathy for Isabel. She had to put up with a lot and she was the mother of his child. I don't have kids. I have no idea what that's all about. But every time I tried to be friendly, within five minutes of being around her, I wanted to sprinkle arsenic on her bagel. It had everything to do with the way she lied.

She's not very clever at it and she does it compulsively. She'll lie about what she had for breakfast. Does anyone care whether she had eggs or pancakes? I think she lies

about this and everything else because controlling information makes her feel safe. But that alone wouldn't be
enough to inspire my arsenic fantasies. Isabel's other annoying habit is that she's always very, very sweet. Sweetness
and lies are my least favorite combination because if you
call the liar on her fallacies she acts like she's the victim.
You end up looking like a bitch because you've attacked
someone who has never been anything but extremely pleas-
ant. At least in Los Angeles that's the case. New Yorkers
wouldn't be slowed down by this charade. Claire, who was
Connecticut by way of Manhattan, had no patience for the
Mother Teresa routine. Every time Isabel talked about how
she had to drive to Santa Barbara to care for her aging Aunt
Maureen who was having a bad asthma day, Claire would
later joke that that was code for I'm blowing some guy at
the beach.

Isabel showed up unannounced. Not only didn't she call
first, she managed to get Gus, the guard at the entrance
to this supposedly private and secure community, to let her
in without clearance from Mr. F.

"I told him it was a birthday surprise."

Mr. F was six months away from his next birthday and
hated surprises, but I let her in. What else could I do?

"Gus is usually not that gullible."

"It's all harmless," she replied as she walked down the
hallway, peering into various rooms as if assessing their
worth. She reminded me of a real estate agent at an open
house, except real estate agents don't usually wear sunglasses and a very expensive silk scarf wrapped around their

head in the style of a princess on the Riviera. It was Isabel's new look. Six months ago she was into bohemian chic, and before that, South Beach/Versace.

"So where is he?" She plopped herself down in the living room, taking a seat on the couch next to an Ellsworth Kelly painting.

I didn't know how to answer that. I didn't want her to go charging into Mr. F's bedroom. But for some reason, whenever I'm around Isabel, I turn into a terrible liar. Maybe I'm intimidated by a real pro. Or maybe lying badly is my protest against a woman who seems to do it for a living. With a slight stutter I said, "He's not available right now."

She removed her sunglasses and looked at me imploringly, as if I were being cruel by withholding information.

"But he is here?"

"I think so."

"Is Anna here?"

Isabel knew that Mr. F's housekeeper never worked weekends.

"She might be," I said, unconvincingly.

Isabel considered all this for a second before jumping up and heading toward the master suite.

"He's asleep," I said, hoping that would stop her. It didn't. I picked up the phone and hit the intercom number for Mr. F's room. But before I got a word out, I heard his voice coming from upstairs.

"What do you want, Isabel?"

"I was worried about you," she replied.

"Why?"

His voice came closer and before I could retreat to the kitchen, suddenly there we all were in the hallway, an uncomfortable trio in the best circumstances, but painfully so in this one. This was the first time Mr. F had come out of his room in days. (Meals had been left outside the door on a tray.) He hadn't shaved and was wearing an old Knicks T-shirt and pajama bottoms. Isabel looked stricken by the sight of him. The nurturing side of her that tended to ailing aunts worked best in stories, not in practice. For a second she actually recoiled from him. It was not a scene I needed to witness. I felt like an interloper who had stumbled into their home movie, and now even if they burned the film, I'd still possess the image.

I tried to sidle past them but Mr. F grabbed my arm while Isabel kept talking. "I've been worried about you. I called three days ago and you never phoned back. You know my seventy-two-hours rule. If I'm still worried about something after seventy-two hours, I have to do something about it. I can't just—"

Mr. F interrupted her as he turned to me. "Lucy, call Gus. Tell him no visitors. None. The drawbridge is not to come down. The crocodiles will stay in the moat and we're keeping them hungry. Gus can issue that as an official warning to any would-be trespassers or he can shoot them. His choice. Got that?"

"Yeah, I got it."

"Repeat it back to me. I want to make sure."

As I complied, I looked over to Isabel. Her eyes were tearing. Of course they were because for the last minute, she'd forced herself not to blink. It's an old acting trick. As

I concluded my recitation, she put her sunglasses on as if trying to cover up the very emotion she'd just conjured up. And then with a quiver in her voice, she touched Mr. F's arm and said, "You need to do yoga."

left them to talk and went to Mr. F's office at the opposite wing of the house. I needed a cigarette and I knew that Anna always stashed a carton in the closet behind a stack of fax paper. In more normal times, Mr. F would have his assistant here five days a week. Lately, there weren't enough calls coming in to keep her busy, so he cut her schedule down to three days, and two weeks ago he sent her away on a paid vacation. Anna and I now used the office as our private escape. In bad weather, we'd come in here to smoke. I'd often find her pretending to clean while the TV set was tuned in to the afternoon soaps, her second favorite addiction after Marlboro Lights.

I found the cigs, lit up and sat in the comfy leather chair behind Mr. F's desk. I gazed out the window surprised at the picture of tranquillity just a few yards away. Oh my God, was that an actual bluebird? Paradise found. Not for long. The fax machine rang and began laboriously spitting out a page. It wasn't my job or business to read it but I did anyway. The privacy I was invading turned out to be my own.

Lucinda baby, I'm keeping my eye on you. I thought you hated going out on a Friday night? You looked good in that dress. Red's your color, baby. So tell the truth. How much do you miss me?

p.s. Did you know two houses on your street were broken into last month?

I knew it was from my ex-boyfriend Matt, though he didn't bother to sign it. He was never big on being accountable for his actions. There was a strong probability that he didn't even send it from his own fax machine. I checked the cover sheet. Kinko's, natch. Call him the king of plausible deniability.

As I reread the note, a chill came over me as if he were spying on me at that very moment. I looked out the window. The bluebird—if it was blue—was gone, the tree branch was still. So was I. An ash fell off the end of my cigarette. I watched it float down onto the pale green rug. I reread the note. I wondered how Matt had gotten Mr. F's fax number. I thought about the lock on my kitchen window, which had been broken for months. Now I'd have to fix it. Fuck that. I'd have to replace it. All locks would have to be changed. Another ash fell as the cigarette burned down closer to my fingers. I could feel the heat as the door opened.

"There you are," Mr. F said. He stood in the doorway as if he were the one intruding. Noticing the fax, he added, "Is that for me? If it is, shred it. It's probably more bad news."

"It's my bad news," I said as I looked around for an ashtray. Finding none, I used the bottom of my shoe to put out the Marlboro and then tossed the butt into an empty wastepaper basket. I handed Mr. F the page.

"My ex has turned into a stalker."

He read it and handed it back to me. "Why?"

"Why? Because he's crazy."

"Everyone's crazy."

"Because he's got too much time on his hands? Because he's got a bizarre sense of humor? Because I bring out the psychotic in men? I don't know." I felt tears coming on, even though I blinked hard to keep them from spilling out in front of my boss. Cynicism came to my rescue.

"I know at least three women who have stalker stories. About a year ago it was very fashionable to have a stalker. If a girl hadn't been to see Gavin de Becker at least once— you know who he is, right? The guy who's the expert on how to deal with obsessed admirers . . . "

"I know who he is."

"Well, for a while there a year ago if you didn't have Gavin on your speed dial you were no one. All the hottest girls had stalkers." It was an exaggeration, but who cares about truth when you're trying to hold on to some kind of emotional equilibrium? I forced my best wiseass smile and craved another cigarette.

Reading my thoughts, he handed me one. "You can stay here if you want. If you don't feel safe going back to your house, stay here in the bunker"—which was how he referred to his home now that he'd become a virtual recluse. There was nothing provocative about the invitation. It was an act of charity, that's all. He and I in the bunker. It was an unlikely combination, the culinary equivalent of a squid and olive salad, which sounded horrible to me until the day I ordered it and discovered it was the kind of thing you could probably acquire a taste for. Over time.

was at the Beverly Glen Market when I found out that the release date for Mr. F's upcoming movie, *Last Standing,* had been pushed back—again. The *Hollywood Reporter* ran the item on its cover. Though it wasn't the day's big headline, the bad news was prominently splashed. I immediately put the paper back on the magazine rack, feeling like a traitor for even reading it in public. The last thing I wanted was to appear concerned, though of course I was. I felt bad for Mr. F. A push back wasn't just a clear message that the picture was in trouble, it was another sign that his fortunes had turned.

Here, having your luck go bad is treated like a symptom of SARS. People may say all the right things, after all Southern California is the home of "have a nice day," but then they'll quickly move away, as if exposure to any kind of harsh reality will dull their own luster and infect their lungs. This is a town where you are who you eat with, so associating with anyone going through a slump is considered practically suicidal.

I, on the other hand, tended to split the loser category into two parts. Actual losers and underdogs. My favorite people in Hollywood are those who have been up and down so many times they make Lazarus look like an amateur. Mr. F may have been out of favor at the moment but I wouldn't/couldn't count him out.

As I replaced the *Reporter*, a hand reached over to grab a copy of the L.A. *Times*.

"Rita?" It was a question because if it was Rita she'd done some serious surgery. Goodbye, bad chin, hello, lipo.

"Lucinda. How are you? I was just thinking about you the other day because I want to get your recipe for that fabulous seafood salad."

"Anytime."

"You still at the same place?"

"Yep. And you? Still working for Daniel?"

She answered by thrusting the newspaper in front of me. "There's my boss." She pointed to the left-hand column on the front page, the column that often is the section for stories about rich people who have been very, very good (huge donation to medical research or buying computers for ghetto schools) or very, very bad (ex-Enron execs or messy divorces that involve six-figure monthly expenses). Daniel Cross, who had made a fortune when he'd sold (but still ran) his independent movie production company, Next Wave Films, to the biggest studio in town, was in the news for being a good guy. He'd given a huge donation to finance a summer sports camp for underprivileged kids. Though it wouldn't have surprised me to see him written up for some prominent nasty dispute. You don't get to be his kind of rich and powerful by being polite. Daniel loved a good fight, and even when he lost a bout or two, he was immune to the label of loser because he was the only one in Hollywood who had somehow come out of every dip in cachet with an upswing that propelled him to even greater heights.

"Saint Daniel," I said as I got to the paragraph that listed the amount of his donation.

"A saint who knows how to party," Rita replied as she added a two-liter bottle of Belvedere vodka to her shopping cart.

We walked out into the parking lot together. My car, the standard model Jeep Cherokee, was parked right out front, next to Rita's ride. An identical model, but newer. It was another peaceful sunny day up on the hill. Life was good up in the Glen. Everyone calmly went about their business, nonchalant even when a famous TV actress was next to them in line at Starbucks. Or an Academy Award winner was breakfasting in the corner booth at the deli. Or a Hollywood legend was having a business meeting over a plate of sashimi at Sushi Ko. There was something so placidly suburban about the place, even with the Hollywood glitz, that accidentally leaning on your car's horn felt like an obscenity.

As I placed my grocery bags in the backseat, Rita went to open the door to her car. "Oh my God," she shrieked, "who keyed you?"

"Who what?"

"Keyed you."

I stepped around to see what she was talking about. Deep scratches, the kind done with a key or a sharp blade, ran from the fender to the headlight and then back again. "I can't fucking believe this."

Rita looked over her shoulder, as if the guilty party might still be lurking around. I did, too, but there was nothing out of the ordinary. A mother with her towheaded twins. An older man putting his dry cleaning in the back of his Mercedes. It was also possible my car had been attacked days before without me realizing it. Since staying up at Mr. F's, I always parked in the garage to the left of the Porsche he rarely drove. I tried to remember the last time I'd glanced at the passenger side.

"Do you think this was a random act of violence?" Rita asked.

"Why would anyone want to key an old Jeep? A brand-new BMW? Maybe. But this isn't exactly the kind of car that inspires hate or envy."

"True," she said. She took a closer look at the damage. "Hope you have a small deductible. This could be expensive."

"Covered," I said.

"That's good."

As she got into her Cherokee I couldn't help but feel as if this incident was an example of my luck, like Mr. F's, also having taken a turn for the worse. Rita put her car in reverse and backed out of her space. Then, shifting into drive, she stuck her hand out the window and gave me a quick wave goodbye. She looked like she was in a big hurry, no doubt with important errands to run and saints to feed.

. . .

r. F insisted on checking out the damage. He came out to the garage wearing sweats, a towel draped around his shoulders, beads of sweat on his brow from his very first yoga class. He stooped down to get a better look and winced. "Fucking yoga fucked up my back."

I resisted the urge to help him up, not wanting to cross any boundaries. I was his chef, not his nurse. Besides, having someone help you stand can make anyone feel eighty. And the last thing a man going through a depression needs is a reminder of what's waiting down the road.

I stooped down next to him. "I don't care how good Christy Turlington looked on that cover of *Vogue*, those pretzel postures are not for me."

He nodded, probably relieved that I wasn't suggesting he work on his breathing and the rest would follow. I've always been good at bonding over politically incorrect opinions. And I wasn't doing it just to suck up to my boss. It was actually possible that we were the only two people in the Beverly Glen zip code who didn't think yoga was a good thing.

He ran his hand along the scratches, which at close range proved to be deep cuts. It was starting to feel personal.

"Did your stalker do this?"

"Matt? My ex?"

"Whatever his name is. Your stalker."

"No!" My denial came fast and emphatically.

"Whoa there, little missy. I'm not accusing, just asking." He delivered the line in the same cowboy drawl he'd used for the movie *Posse*.

Using the car for leverage, he pushed himself upright.

I continued to stare at the damage, which was making me nauseous. "Why did you say Matt? Do you think he'd do something like this?"

"I've never met the man."

"So why did you guess Matt?" Even as I insisted on an answer, I was aware that I was becoming one of those annoying people who prodded someone into saying what I was thinking so I could deny it was true.

Mr. F took the towel from around his neck, twisted it and playfully whacked me over the head. "You're fucked up. I don't know what your Dr. Davenport is telling you but you've got a few problems."

I stood up and leaned against my car. I was already exhausted just thinking about dealing with the insurance company, deductibles, repairs, and my increasing paranoia. "I haven't seen Dr. Davenport in a while. Can't afford him." And then before Mr. F could offer another opinion of my mental health, I quickly changed the subject.

"Want some lunch?"

I made turkey burgers and salad. Wheat buns on the side. I didn't know if Mr. F was on or off the no wheat/no dairy diet, so I always provided options. This time, he went for the whole thing, including mayo, lettuce, pickles and tomatoes. I wondered if there were any men anywhere who lost their appetite when they were depressed, or if that was just a girl thing. Lately it seemed I was cooking more but eating less. Stressed out about my own life, I could eat only half a burger, no bread and a bite of salad. I also felt self-conscious eating in front of my boss. It felt weird to be both the cook and the guest but he'd insisted I join him. Guess

he was getting a little lonely up in the bunker, so I did my
best to keep a conversation going.

"This is progress. You're out of your room. You actually
took a yoga class."

Well, it wasn't a class exactly, it was a private session. His
first. He'd considered yoga a few months earlier but ruled
it out because he said it was "too granola" for him, and that
if he was going to go Eastern, he was going to go Bruce Lee
martial arts, not lotus position.

"Add that to the list of things I won't do again. Won't be
going to any shrinks, won't be standing on my head."

"But you actually let a stranger in here. And one with a
turban on his head. That's something."

Another one for the list. "Won't be letting Isabel send
over any of her A-team."

That was Mr. F's term for his ex's team of experts. She
had quite a collection. Yoga teacher. Masseuse. Psychic.
Every kind of doctor imaginable. As well as a spiritual ad-
visor she referred to as her "life coach."

He leaned back and reached for a large, black leather-
bound appointment book that was on the countertop next
to the phone. He tossed it down on the table in front of me.

"Cancel them all," he said.

It took me a moment before I realized he wasn't just
ranting and actually expected me to cancel his appointments. "All of them?"

"All. Not reschedule. Cancel."

As I flipped through the pages, I saw what no action
hero wants his fans to see. Appointments for facials. Tanning sessions. Pedicures. Bi-monthly visits from his hair-

dresser. And, most incriminating of all, the name of the surgeon best known for doing liposuction. It was not a pretty picture so I quickly closed the book.

"Well, at least you're not locked inside your bedroom with the blackout shades down."

Mr. F pulled on the beard that he'd grown over the last week. He was starting to remind me a little of a college professor I once fucked.

"Ever been to the Cape?"

Lost in my erotic flashback, it took me a moment to make any sense out of his question.

"Which cape? Aren't there a bunch of them? Cape Anne?"

"Cod," he said. "Cape Cod. I grew up there."

"Oh right. I think I read that somewhere."

"Not the ritzy part."

I had no idea where he was going with any of this. "No, haven't been. Was supposed to go to Martha's Vineyard once but it was the same week Clinton was there—this is when he was president—and I didn't relish having my vacation held up by a presidential motorcade."

"There will be no motorcades in Falmouth."

"Great."

"So, you want to come with me?"

Funny how slight changes in wording alter everything. Not that I thought he was inviting me as his date, but this was something other than a statement or request to an employee. That would have sounded more like this: "I'll need you to come with me." Or, "Do you have a problem with traveling to such and such?" When I was first hired, he mentioned I might have to come along on location if he rented a house and needed a chef.

"Is this a vacation?" I asked, stalling for time.

"More like a temporary relocation."

I didn't know what to say. I didn't even know if I had a choice. Was it relocation or no location?

"Or you can stay in L.A. with your stalker."

It wasn't a threat. In fact Mr. F smiled, possibly the first smile I'd seen from him since the Claire incident.

"How long are you thinking of relocating?"

"I'm thinking two weeks."

"Two weeks. Oh that's fine. I thought you meant like six months or something."

"When have I ever committed to anything for six months?"

He had a point.

eight

You're thinking you see where this is going—it's a
Jane Eyre/Mr. Rochester scenario. You are wrong,
wrong, wrong. Mr. Famous was only attracted to
women who dazzled him, and it's hard to dazzle when
you're chopping onions and sweating over large pots of boil-
ing pasta. And that was fine with me. I admit that I used to
think he was sexy about a decade ago when he was a lot
more rock 'n' roll. And I also have to admit that five years
ago, in the movie *Countdown*, I was captivated watching
him save the galaxy from annihilation. Though the blond
highlights in his hair were a bad choice, making him look
a little like Ryan Seacrest or some surfer-deejay past his
prime. Even as recently as three years ago, I was charmed
when introduced to him at a small party I catered for his
friend Lawrence. But I can never sustain interest in someone who shows no signs of lust for me. I can obsess over an
un-getable guy only if I'm sleeping with him. Besides, I've
always hated Jane Eyre. She's a classic passive-aggressive.
The twenty-first-century version plays nurse to some rich

guy in rehab. Without asking for a thing, she gets him to believe his recovery is inextricably connected to her beneficent
presence in his life. And then once she's got him to make
that connection, she's in. Another spiritual gold digger finds
a fancy home. There are a lot of recovering Rochesters in
Hollywood and just as many Janes waiting for them to walk
out of Betty Ford.

The night before Mr. Famous and I were to leave for the
Cape, I made a date to see Lou, who was the closest
thing I had to a boyfriend since splitting up with Matt. We
could best be described as friends who fuck, except every so
often we got a little territorial. If he got a call from a girl
while I was over there, I might sulk. If I got a call from a
guy while we were at my place, he might start kissing my
stomach (my most ticklish spot) to get me to hang up. But
most of the time it was a straightforward deal. Fun sex. No
expectations. Connection without attachment. Sometimes I
felt like a fucking Zen Buddhist. But then I realized that the
only reason I could be so detached was because I was attached elsewhere. I was attached to the notion that I was not
going to settle for just any relationship—even if that meant
living alone for the rest of my life. It's amazing how many
women resented me for this. Especially women stuck in
dull relationships. It could get ugly. They called me a snob.
A deluded snob. Hollywood is a small town. Their comments got back to me. "Who does she think she's going to
get? It's not like she's Angelina Jolie." I've fantasized fax-
ing all these catty women a cartoon that ran in *The New
Yorker*. Two women walking down the street, talking. Nei-

ther looks happy. The caption reads: I have a significant other but he sucks.

The thing about Lou is that he was in sync with me on this issue. He was mid-thirties and wasn't tempted by a relationship unless it was with some spectacular girl, and his definition of spectacular was Pamela Anderson's looks with Christiane Amanpour's brains. Kids and fear—two reasons a lot of men end up settling for someone less than their ideal—were not factors yet. So he and I checked in with each other occasionally—and even jokingly referred to each other as girlfriend/boyfriend.

The sex always worked. Always. There wasn't one misfire. There was great comfort in knowing we fit together so well, but Lou also kept things from getting too predictable. Sex with him was often an adventure, and his comments could be surprising and delightful. One time we were lounging on his bed, naked, sweaty, and he turned to me and said, "You have a very sexy waist." My body falls into the category of athletic, but I do happen to have a perfect waist. However, when you live in a tits-and-ass culture, no one even notices. Lou definitely scored points for being the rare exception.

Cape fucking Cod? Who goes there unless it's summer and even then?" Lou was smoking some weed as we lazed around, the TV on in the background.

"That's the point. To go someplace quiet."

He shrugged. He didn't understand and he didn't care all that much. We weren't big talkers. It wasn't part of our deal. And we never discussed anything serious. Maybe I'd mentioned my ex-boyfriend Matt once. Just in passing. And

I certainly didn't reveal that Matt might be a potential stalker.

Lou didn't drag me into any of his dramas either. I knew he worked for a production company that made videos and commercials. In addition to our bodies fitting, our psychological cases matched up. We were both terrified of emotional intimacy. Of course this was never discussed because that would be too intimate. It was tacit. We kept things on an easygoing level.

He offered me the joint. "What will you do there?"

I declined his offer because Lou smoked some pretty potent stuff and I still had to pack for the trip. "I'll cook Mr. F's meals."

"That doesn't take all day."

"I don't know. I'll take up knitting." It was an idea that came to me out of nowhere. I didn't even know where one bought yarn. But the image of me on a chilly evening, sitting in front of a fire, knitting a scarf for the boyfriend I didn't have, seemed oddly comforting.

Of course Lou knew girls who were knitters but they were all twenty. They did it on the set of videos to get attention, believing that aspiring actresses who knit were viewed as more serious. Only in Hollywood could knitting get you the same credit as reading Tolstoy.

"I had a girl make me a sweater once, she put the buttons on the wrong side," he said.

Something about that sentence summed up everything.

I didn't respond. I focused on the TV—reruns of "The Larry Sanders Show" on Bravo.

At the commercial break, Lou stroked my arm. "We've had fun, don't you think?"

"Yeah," I replied, wondering if the "had" meant that we were moving into the permanent past tense. I was only going away for two weeks so there was no reason to feel like this was winding down, so why did it feel like goodbye?

When I got to the entrance of Mr. F's "private community," there was an old silver-gray BMW driving out. I recognized the driver as Stephanie, a girl Mr. F occasionally saw. She was his version of Lou; unfortunately, she wasn't going along with his program. Stephanie wanted more. She'd take Mr. F in a depression. She'd take Mr. F in a coma as long as there was some reason to hope that down the line she could close the deal. She wanted to be attached to someone with a name. That was her vocation. She was pretty and she was willing to wait. Maybe not forever, but definitely until his next film was released. Mr. F perpetuated a vague promise of something more because she gave great blow jobs and was relatively low maintenance. This info didn't come from him but from her. Stephanie prided herself on these two "talents." As I said, it's a small town and word gets around.

As Gus opened the security fence and waved me in, Stephanie and I passed each other. I'd met her a few times and was prepared to wave hello, but she sped past me as if she was above acknowledging the help. I did get a glimpse of Gus in my rearview mirror. He was shaking his head and grinning as if to say, This is how movie stars live. Women coming and going around the clock. The myth was still alive even if it was only with the gatekeeper.

nine

During the winter months, five o'clock was the darkest hour of the day for Mr. F. That January evening was no exception. He knew why. It had started when he was a kid. Three days a week, he'd leave basketball practice around five and start the trek across the schoolyard and through the poorly lit park that ended at the border of his neighborhood. Every sound, every shadowy figure walking behind him felt like a threat. His parents were too beaten up by life and too wrapped up in caring for his crippled brother to worry about how their youngest son got home. In their defense, it was a more innocent time. But that didn't lessen the anxiety Mr. F felt for the entire twelve minutes (he'd timed it) it took to walk through the park. It was during one of those walks that he had his first real testosterone moment—one he'd ended up drawing on for some of his most successful action flicks.

On that particular night, when he was about halfway into the park—the darkest section—he saw in the distance, coming toward him, a guy who was clearly bigger and walked with an intimidating swagger. Mr. F immediately considered his exit options. Veer off to the left, run as fast as he could and hope that he made it to the brightly lit State Avenue before he was tackled. Or, retreat back to where he came from, in the hope of running into someone else (reinforcements) who might be heading back from practice.

Not for a second did he consider that the approaching stranger could be harmless. For a moment he was frozen, unable to decide on a course of action. As the figure neared, Mr. F saw that he was dressed in the black jacket and black jeans uniform that the gang over on Doran Street favored. He felt his heart beating fast, knocking so hard he actually knocked back, pounding on his own chest as if to say quiet down in there.

It was time to flee or face the consequences. And at that moment, a voice in him arose from the rebellious spirit he didn't even know he possessed and said NO. No. No. No. NO. He looked around for a rock, a branch, any kind of weapon. There was nothing on the ground except some discarded candy wrappers. And the voice continued . . . "No. No. No fucking way. Not going to happen. NO. NO. Not this time. Not again." As the voice in his head got louder, he started to walk toward the stranger. At some point his hands came out of his pockets. His gaze shifted up from the ground. The hulk of a figure was only ten yards away. Mr. F's walk slowed. Not to delay the inevitable but to better prepare for it. He started to hit the side of his own leg, as he was too wound up to keep his fist quiet. A sound started to gurgle up from his throat. With every exhale, it got louder. Five yards away now. Mr. F locked his eyes on the guy's face. No one he knew but he recognized the type. Tough, angry guy with steel-toe boots. Mr. F came to that conclusion without checking out the guy's footwear. No way was he going to look away. No way was he going to blink first. Three yards away. The guy glared back and kept glaring even after he passed Mr. F. As he looked over his shoulder, he mumbled something that sounded like "Fucking whack job."

Mr. F didn't reply or comment. He didn't care if he'd been dissed. All that mattered was that he'd rattled this thug. He couldn't believe he had it in him to be intimidating. Beyond that, to be considered dangerous. He'd never even considered aggressiveness as a defense before. It was a turning point. It was a whole new Mr. F. Except he never did completely dispel the lingering sense of darkness and loneliness that the five P.M. winter hour evoked. Not even almost thirty-five years later.

He took the call even though he was in no mood to talk. It was from Alex, who in his inimitable agent style got right to the point.

"Robert Kaye doesn't like the movie."

Kaye was the studio exec who had greenlit the project. His negative reaction was no surprise since he was a guy known for knowing nothing. He had no meaningful opinion because all he went by was what marketing said. In spite of his lack of credibility, the vote still stung. Mr. F almost came right out and admitted it. One step away from asking . . . Why doesn't rejection by a moron feel like a good thing? That would be too philosophical and too honest, so he went with a little sarcasm. "What doesn't he like about it? Too intelligent for him?"

Alex didn't laugh. "Robert didn't get into what or why. All he said was they might need some reshoots. What's your availability?"

Mr. F looked out through the French doors to the darkened patio. One of the outdoor lights wasn't working. He hated when that happened. "We'll talk availability after he apologizes to the girl in craft services. The one he screamed at the day he visited the set. I want him on his knees. Then we'll talk reshoots."

Mr. F was not usually so uncooperative, nor was he usually all that aware or protective of the service crews. But Robert Kaye was a leverage abuser of the first order, and now that he was an abuser and also not a fan of the movie, Mr. F wasn't opposed to throwing his own leverage around.

Alex sighed. He had no time for this. "Don't be crazy. I'll call you tomorrow morning." He was already on to another call, while Mr. F still held the phone in his hand. He wasn't crazy. It was just that hour of the winter evening, and for a moment he was twelve again.

ten

When the plane touched down at Logan Airport in Boston it was snowing lightly. I'm not a fan of cold weather, neither is Mr. F. It was March, almost spring, not that that means anything in New England, where snow on an Easter Sunday is taken in stride.

As we got off the plane, Mr. F attracted stares. He was wearing a baseball-style cap with the letter V on it and Italian-made wraparound sunglasses. I'm not sure if people recognized him or stared because he commanded attention. Despite his fragile ego, he had the walk of a VIP.

It was the first time I had ever been in a crowded public place with my boss. I have to admit I did consider the possibility that one of our fellow travelers might have a camera and get off a few uncontested snapshots of the two of us. Worse, I imagined that photo ending up in some tabloid. And much worse and even harder to admit, I immediately straightened out my scarf and fluffed out my hair, just in case.

J.J., the guy from the car service, met us at the gate. He

had a strong Boston accent and talked too fast and too much about the traffic and the weather. Mr. Famous gave him nothing back. Not a nod, not a smile, nothing. I felt bad for J.J. Maybe this was his first big celebrity passenger. I also felt protective of my boss. I didn't want people going around saying he was a dick. So I picked up the slack and discussed turnpikes and the five-day forecast until we reached baggage claim and J.J. gave us the keys, pointed to where the limo was parked across the street and stayed behind to gather our luggage.

The snow was now turning to rain, which didn't help much. It was still gray skies above and slush on the ground, and it was hard not to wonder what the fuck we were doing there, shoulders hunched against the wind, ears turning red. How could this possibly help anyone's depression— especially anyone who five and a half hours earlier had left behind a perfect California day.

Mr. F unlocked the car and got into the driver's seat. He turned on the ignition to get some heat going. I sat in the back and reached for a bottle of Evian. That was it. No alcohol. No snacks. Just water. Not exactly equipped for a VIP, and I was starving. Cold and hungry in a limo is still cold and hungry.

Mr. F turned on the radio and flipped through several stations, giving each one no more than a few seconds before moving on. Finally he snapped it off. He took off his baseball cap and checked out his hair in the rearview mirror. He fiddled with a few graying strands that stuck out from his receding hairline, also giving that effort no more than a moment before slapping the cap back on. Ignoring me, he then stared straight ahead, not that there was anything to see. The limo was parked on the ground level of a semi-enclosed parking structure. Maybe his antisocial mood was a good thing, I decided. Hopefully, he was calculating how quickly we could head back to the West Coast. At that moment I would have gladly traded bleak Boston for sunny L.A., even if that came with a stalker.

Eventually I turned around and saw through the back window that J.J. was approaching, managing all four bags with an ease that suggested he was used to hard labor. I got out to help him anyway, just to have something to do and because Mr. Famous hadn't said a word for fifteen minutes and it was starting to freak me out.

The first hour of the trip was uneventful. My boss and I were now both in the backseat and we were at least talking. After several failed attempts at discussing current events or sports—the Celtics were actually doing okay this season—we ended up like addicts going back to the one thing we could count on to distract us from real life— Hollywood.

"Why don't journalists ever bust these girls on their bull-shit?" The question was inspired by the cover of one of the magazines I'd brought with me. The girl I was referring to was an actress known for saying provocative things that were often, if not a total lie, a gross exaggeration. "I've never had plastic surgery." "I've never had a guy dump me." "I'm not interested in marriage."

I handed Mr. Famous the article. "Look at that photo. That's not her real nose. And I know two guys who have dumped her, and she proposed to one of them."

He glanced at the photograph, didn't even bother to scan the interview. "Oh, her. She's okay. Not my type but harmless."

"Harmless? The girl's a role digger. She'll fuck anyone to get a good part. Why doesn't someone bust her on her skanky past? Since when did journalism become a career for sycophants?"

Mr. Famous pulled the brim of his hat down farther as if it were a sombrero and he was getting ready for a siesta. "What's the upside for one of those magazines to bust anyone? If you start busting people, they'll start watching everything they say. Facts don't matter. Good copy matters."

"Ah, I see," I said, trying not to show how riled up I could get about these issues. Being argumentative wasn't in my job description. "You're giving me the 'that's entertainment' argument. I might have to get you to watch *Quiz Show*." I'd recently rented the movie on DVD and totally related to the Rob Morrow character, who was trying to get a Congressional committee to act in the interest of the culture, not the corporations. (I was so much more pragmatic when I was younger. Why was my rebellious period hitting me now that I was in my thirties?)

Mr. Famous looked out the window, though there was nothing to see along this stretch of road except trees and exit ramps. "I saw it when it came out. I like Bob Redford but he needs to lighten up on some of his issues."

"You sound like the Geritol guy."

"What? What do you mean, Geritol?"

Even with his "sombrero" pulled down, I could see his look of concern. I think he thought I was accusing him of being old.

"Geritol," I explained, "was the sponsor of the quiz show in *Quiz Show*. Marty Scorsese played the Geritol exec whose attitude was 'It's entertainment. It's a game.' "

"He's right."

"If it's all just a game, how come no one's having fun?"

Mr. Famous took a second and then broke into a big hearty laugh. I took it as a compliment, thinking my wit was sharper than I thought, until he stopped abruptly and said, "Is that what you want?"

Though not an Oscar-caliber actor, I have to say Mr. Famous knew how to deliver a convincing laugh on cue.

"Impressive," I said.

The approval cheered him up. I can only imagine what a round of applause might have accomplished.

We decided to get something to eat. J.J. took the first exit, which brought us to a factory town in southeastern Massachusetts. The rain had stopped. The skies were clearing but I felt even more depressed. Bankrupt factory towns are not pretty. From the highway they have a certain charm—all those picturesque church steeples and smokestacks—but when you're down in it, driving through the streets, no one over twelve looks happy. When we got to the center of town it was like entering a time warp. Street after street of run-down stores displaying merchandise that looked like it was from an old Spiegel catalog. You could really age fast here, I thought.

I couldn't help but get into some serious California dreaming. I was aching for it the way you do for a lover you broke up with—for good reasons—but then miss so much you'll do anything to get him back. Offer blow jobs on demand. Agree to an open relationship. Go to hockey games. I'm not saying it's healthy, I'm just saying it happens.

J.J. kept driving around, slowing down as we passed any place that looked like it served food.

"I think we just found a city with no restaurants. Is that a *Guinness Book of World Records* kind of thing?" I wasn't counting coffee shops or Burger Kings. Admittedly, I was a food snob, but I would have settled for some place that had a real salad on the menu.

J.J. tried another side street and slowed down in front of an establishment called Roy's, a Chinese restaurant with mustard-colored curtains in the window. The place appeared closed but had a sign out front that said OPEN. Of course the sign looked like it had been there for a century. Prospects for a real salad were diminishing when Mr. Famous's cell phone rang.

He answered it, though not before checking to see the incoming number. "What's up, Alex?"

I watched his face, as much of it as I could see beneath his cap, as he listened to his agent's news. It didn't look like he was being offered the lead role in Ridley Scott's next film.

"Is that right?" He listened to Alex's response for a few seconds before cutting him off. "I don't give a fuck about down the line."

I could imagine Alex trying to be reasonable on the other end but Mr. F was having none of it. "Got to go," he said and powered off. He then buzzed down the window and tossed his cell phone out into the street. I watched it land in a small pool of slush near the curb and then slide into a gutter.

By way of explanation he simply said, "They've taken *Last Standing* off the release schedule."

It was the kind of news item that would depress any actor whether or not his performance had anything to do with the decision. Doesn't matter. In Hollywood, not taking things personally is something you say, not do.

I had the strongest urge to touch his arm reassuringly, but I was his chef not his girlfriend. So I tried to reassure him with the usual platitudes. "This business is run by morons. Studio executives have no guts. Every actor I know has been sabotaged by the system one time or another. Comes with the territory. No big deal." Though of course it was.

All I got back was silence. An oppressive, thick silence. Poor J.J. He didn't know what to do. He kept the car double parked and idling in front of the Chinese restaurant.

"You want to try this place?" he finally asked. His question was addressed to me because Mr. Famous, in his dark tunnel of silence, was scary.

I looked out the window, and then down to the end of the block where a sign above a doorway caught my attention.

"How about that place? Right there on the corner?"

"That's not a restaurant."

"That's right, it's not."

I put a bottle of tequila, a large bag of chips and a small jar of salsa on the counter and pulled out my credit card. The young man behind the register at Ed's liquor store turned it over to see if I'd signed the card. I hadn't. He took it anyway.

"Want to see my license?" I asked.

He ran the total through the system. "No," he said as he waited for the approval to come through. I don't think my honest face inspired his nonchalance. He was just too tired to give a fuck.

"You don't happen to sell any limes, do you?"

"There's a market two blocks over. We just have those three shelves of food items."

In addition to the chips/salsa selections, Ed's also sold instant coffee, Coffee-mate, sugar and cookies. The card was approved and my purchases bagged.

"Wait," I said, as I pulled a couple of bucks out of my pocket. "Add a package of Oreos." They were for J.J. I figured the guy could use a treat.

Mr. F and I got a little drunk, though not in a sloppy or sexy way. All we did was talk and share a few laughs. I felt like his drinking buddy, and sometimes in life—and this was one of those times—a pal is better company than a lover.

As we drove into the night and toward his hometown, Mr. F helped himself to a couple more swigs of tequila and offered up a few stories. Most of them were nostalgic childhood tales, but when we passed a run-down restaurant bar called the Martinique on Route 6, he changed his tone.

"Go back," he ordered J.J.

I could see J.J.'s confused expression in the rearview mirror. "Back where?" Given Mr. F's changing moods, it could mean back to Logan Airport.

"Back to that place you just passed. The Seaside Lounge."

J.J. did a swift U-turn and stopped in front of a building with a wood-shingled facade and a pink neon sign. Once, it might have had some kind of curb appeal, but now it had become just another generic highway joint where the best travelers could hope for was hot food and cold brew.

As the limo came to a stop, Mr. F opened his window. The smell of deep-fried something filled the air. He seemed to enjoy it. He took a big whiff, and then another as if he were inhaling a tropical ocean breeze. Would he insist we go inside for a little grease and some beer to chase the tequila? It was possible. Thankfully, after a few moments of what appeared to be deep contemplation, he put up his window and said, "Okay. Keep going, Ray."

J.J. didn't correct him and neither did I. J.J.? Ray? Did it really matter at that point? It would be like correcting the grammar of someone who was having trouble getting out a sentence.

After a few more miles, and a few more swigs of tequila, Mr. Famous loosened up. "When I was a teenager, my uncle owned the Seaside Lounge. It was a front for the Providence mob. I thought that was cool. He was the only member of my family who didn't work in a factory. And he always had hot women. I remember this one girl he was really into. She was gorgeous, wanted to be a dancer. She was like that girl in *Flashdance*, but this was before the movie."

"Jennifer Beals?"

"Yeah, her."

"And she was good. I saw her perform once. She was part of some dance company that did a show over in New Bedford. My uncle brought me to see it. He was real proud of her that night but he could also be a son of a bitch. A few months later they were in a fight and he said, 'You're already twenty-six. A dancer's career is over at thirty. What kind of fucking miracle do you think is going to happen between now and then?' He annihilated her with that."

"Yeah, well, the truth can do that," I said.

"Aren't you compassionate?"

"I'm better than compassionate. I'm hopeful. I believe there's life after broken dreams." I got no response to that declaration. Either Mr. F didn't hear or didn't think it warranted a comment. If he were in better shape he might have teased me, saying I was beginning to think and talk like a broken-down Hollywood cliché. He'd be right.

Another ten minutes went by before conversation was resumed. In the meantime, Mr. Famous had taken off the baseball cap. When the car passed through a section of Route 6 that was especially well lit, I saw that he looked exhausted and sad, and just looking at him made me sad. I had to find a distraction.

"What happened to your uncle?"

"He killed himself. Blew his brains out."

Right idea, wrong topic. "Sorry," I said.

"Want to hear the good part of the story?"

"Uh, sure."

"My mother, his sister, was a devout Catholic. Went to church every day but, you know, loved the TV sets and cars her brother gave her. You got to understand, everyone in the neighborhood knew my uncle was a hit man for the mob, but my mother couldn't deal with that. So she convinced herself he made all that money 'cause he had a good head for the restaurant business. One day, he got into big trouble with the IRS. They're about to ship him off to one of the toughest prisons in the state. For all kinds of reasons, he couldn't deal with that. So, BANG. You know what my mother said when she found out? 'Where did he get the gun?' You believe that? Where did he get the gun? How about his glove compartment, Mom?"

J.J. burst out laughing.

Mr. Famous smiled. See, see, Ray gets it. Life can be miserable and hilarious all at the same time. And at that moment, though Mr. F didn't have that exact combination going for himself, at least momentarily his misery had been tempered by a good punch line.

The rain started again, pounding the car hard, making me feel as if I were encapsulated. No matter what we discussed, and the discussions were intermittent, we always worked our way back to Hollywood. A discussion about the lack of justice in show biz led me to ask this question. "Have you ever wished there was a real Don Corleone and he owed you a favor?"

"Everybody has revenge fantasies." His words were slightly slurred so I reopened the bag of chips and offered it to him. He waved it away, possibly not wanting food to interfere with his buzz. He did tightly close the tequila bottle and then stuck it in the magazine pouch behind the driver's seat.

"Tell me one of yours," I persisted. "Don't use real names. I don't need to know." Actually I would have loved to know, but being with a big celebrity required some precautions. As nice as J.J. was, who's to say he wouldn't call up *The Enquirer* ten seconds after he dropped us off.

Mr. F lapsed into another ten minutes of silence before he began his story, which he delivered, in spite of fatigue, booze, jet lag and not one bite of decent food all day, as if an invisible director had just yelled roll and this was the first shot of the day.

"When I was twenty-two, about a year after I came to L.A., a guy I knew from acting class took me to a BBQ at this rich lady's house. A woman about forty. I had had a tough year but it started looking like things were turning around. I'd had three callbacks for a role on a new series. Small part, but a series. I saw big things in my future. I saw myself moving up from renting a room to renting an apartment. I had a feeling I was going to get the part. My agent said they'd let me know for sure on Monday. So that Saturday, I go to the BBQ and have a few beers. Early celebrating. Who's there but one of the producers of the show I'm up for. Turns out she's best friends with rich lady. She gives me a very friendly hello. Big smile on her face and I'm thinking this job's in the bag. Couple of hours go by and rich lady and I end up talking, and I got to give it to her, she wasn't a looker but she was a lot of fun. Smart. Knew a lot about football. Especially the Forty-niners. We got along great and I'm feeling like I've arrived. Chatting up big shots at a catered party. So she says, 'I want to show you my new car.' I say, 'Oh yeah, okay, where is it?' She refills our margaritas and says, 'In the garage.'

"It was a nice top-of-the-line Mercedes. A white one, though. I'm not into white cars but I act all impressed. She says, 'Why don't you get in?' Something about the leather seats. Okay, I go along with it. She gets in, too, and then all of a sudden, she jumps on me."

"Wait," I whispered to Mr. F, as I held up my hand to get him to stop. "Hey, J.J.," I said.

No response, maybe because he knew what was coming. "Hey, J.J., can we have some music?"

He grudgingly turned on the radio and went with the station with the best reception. An oldies station. The Ronettes.

"That's fine. And a little louder."

Phil Spector's wall of sound was even better than a glass partition.

"Okay, boss, continue. I'm listening."

Mr. F pulled me closer and spoke so softly and quickly it was like a bad cell phone connection. I only got every third word. I did get the part about how the woman wanted to be fucked hard and go back into the party wet.

I'd heard this same story before from a professional tennis player, and a similar story from a bartender who once lived across the hall from me. That's the thing about Hollywood. Bits and pieces of the same story keep popping up in different people's bios. Was it coincidence or plagiarism? Not that it mattered. After living in the land of make-believe for a while, truth starts to feel as outdated as dial phones.

"That's a line I'll have to try out," I said sarcastically.

"Hey," he said somewhat defensively. "I've fucked women I haven't been that into but there was something about this one—too hungry. I couldn't do it. There's hot, there's hot and hungry, and then there's just hungry."

"So let me guess. Monday comes and you don't get the job 'cause she trashed you to her friend the producer."

"So much for a surprise ending."

"It's the AW network," I said, as I dropped the whispering. "Angry Women. I worked for one of them once. While I was making dinner she'd be on the phone in the kitchen, talking to her girlfriends as if I weren't there, openly planning the demise of some guy who rejected them. Of course the guy had to be struggling. If he had any power at all, they'd pretend the rejection never happened and be all 'Hi, doll' the next time they saw him."

J.J. upped the sound on the radio just a bit. Guess he didn't give a fuck about angry women or maybe he just liked the song. It was one of my favorite INXS songs. Could have been on Mr. F's hit list as well, because suddenly all talking ceased.

As I listened to Michael Hutchence's sexy voice, I thought about how people are always gushing about the love of their life. What about the lust of their life? Isn't that as monumental? Hutchence sure made it sound irresistible. And though love and lust often go together when you're eighteen, it gets harder to find as you get older. I thought about what it must be like for a movie star who has so many options for both, and I wondered at what point does pursuing lust without love become unseemly and at worst destructive. On the other hand, if you subscribed to the theory that sex was an elixir, it could be equally destructive to choose love at the price of lust. It was difficult enough for me to figure out and I didn't have anywhere near the choices that come with fame. I did know one thing, though. Hollywood was all about survival of the fittest, and any true Darwinian would tell you that nature is not kind to those who don't adapt to new situations.

J.J. pulled up to a small quaint Cape Cod–style inn. White shingles. Black shutters. Front porch. "We're here," he announced triumphantly.

I got out of the car as J.J. popped open the trunk. I grabbed two bags and carried them up to the front entrance. Mr. Famous walked up to the porch steps and stopped to lean on the banister, seemingly oblivious to the rain pouring down. He took a good look at the place, appraising it the way you might study the face of an old friend you haven't seen for years, trying to get a sense of how life had treated them.

I worried he was either too focused on his appraisal or too out of it in general to deal with J.J., so I did.

"Do we need to sign anything?"

"Nope. All taken care of."

He hesitated for a second and then without another word to me, he approached Mr. Famous. Tentatively. "It's been a true pleasure driving you, sir. I'm a big fan."

"Thanks, Ray," Mr. F said and then, almost as an afterthought, smiled.

Again J.J. didn't bother to correct him on the name, he was just so damned excited that he'd just shaken the hand of a movie star.

Typical, I thought. I'm the one who bought him cookies and laughed at his bad jokes about weather and turnpikes.

Yet he doesn't even say goodbye to me. I could have saved his fucking life and at the end of the ride all he'd care about was whether he had a moment with the big guy. I was beginning to see that when you're around a big celebrity, people either acknowledge you because you're part of their world, or you're completely invisible. I'm not sure which is worse, and with that thought I grabbed two more of the suitcases out of the trunk and went inside. Mr. F followed, ignoring the remaining luggage on the front porch, assuming someone else would carry them in. And of course someone else did.

eleven

Mr. Famous wasn't in the mood to work out but forced himself into the gym. His gym. Bottom floor, left wing of the house. Despite the convenience, he hated having a gym at home. It ruined the aesthetic for him. Gyms didn't belong in houses the same way television sets didn't belong in living rooms. It was an elitist position to take but he'd take inconvenience over crassness any day—if he could. But being a movie star deprived him of the choice. What was the option—go to Gold's Gym and work out with the masses?

He turned on the TV that was built into a wall unit directly in front of the cardio equipment. Local news. He picked up a pair of free weights and started in on a set of bicep curls. In many ways he missed the big noisy gym on Cole Street. Before he got too famous he enjoyed being around other people pushing for their personal best. It inspired him. But after his first summer blockbuster, it was less about camaraderie and more about sweating for an audience. People would halt their own workout to stare at him.

And then there were the women. Tempting. Available. Thrilled to talk to him. Easy. Easy. Easy. And he'd done it too many times. He'd dated a number of the ones he'd met at Gold's and at the start it was all good. But in each and every case it ended up in the same place—with the girl telling him he was bad for her self-esteem. And he was, if her self-esteem depended on him to be monogamous and in love with her. What did they think would happen? He wished someone would educate them to the fact that they were not on a level playing field. He was a movie star and they were a personal trainer, or aspiring actress, or junior agent or waitress/singer. He was always careful not to mislead them with any romantic stuff, but these girls seemed not to notice. By the third date they were confessing their love for him, which they expressed as if it were a prize, not a burden. It made for an awkward moment. Plus, once a woman declared her love—this was the part that really annoyed him—she felt a greater connection had been established, which made her more comfortable asking for favors. Money for her car insurance. Help on getting into a casting. Advice about her small claims court case against a drycleaners who ruined the Gucci shirt that she got on sale at Neiman's and couldn't replace. And if he didn't help them out, they reacted as if he'd kicked a homeless person in the head and stolen their shoes. They would be astonished that "he wasn't there for them," especially since he was so blessed and they were struggling. He came close to saying, First of all, this "I love you/you owe me" approach? Doesn't work with me. And secondly, we all have problems.

When you get down to it, pumping iron is pumping iron no matter how much money you have in the bank and how many people know your name. But they'd end up missing the point and instead misquote him so it sounded as if he were saying there was no difference between living in a hovel and working out in your private gym up in your Bel Air mansion. At least Claire had her own money—well, her family's. And if anything, she had an inflated sense of her worth. So much so that she declared that she was a boost to his self-esteem. Most of the time he admired her for her confidence, but occasionally, just occasionally, it intimidated him.

The news anchor on channel 4 was reporting another story about a politician's statement on such and such. Who cares? These guys changed their position every day. Mr. F hated the big rat fuck of it all. He couldn't stand to listen to these politicians bullshit so earnestly. At least people in Hollywood knew how to bullshit and entertain. They understood that earnestness only works for one scene in the third act. And when it comes to action movies—maybe one line in the third act. Action heroes keep it simple. They keep it clean.

A few movies ago he played a soldier of fortune who had to rescue a senator's son. The senator was one of those politicians who had all the answers to all the wrong questions, but didn't know shit about the way the world actually worked outside Capitol Hill. At the end of the film he got to confront the senator in a kind of "you can't handle the truth" moment, except it was set on an airstrip in South

America and Mr. F had an automatic rifle in his hand and had just saved the day by killing six members of the dictator's death squad. It was one of his favorite performances and he wondered why it wasn't airing on cable more often.

He put down the free weights and picked up the remote. He flipped off channel 4 and tuned into an entertainment news show. As he arranged himself on the bench to press his daily quota, he listened to an inane reporter gush about the latest reconciliation of a Hollywood couple. It was like gushing over a metronome. The couple had broken up and gotten back together so many times Mr. F couldn't believe anyone cared. He knew the actress would never walk away from this guy for long. He was a respected director and her last job was a small guest spot on *Charmed*. This girl was never going to stray far from any guy who had big heat, even if the relationship was killing her. She wanted fame so bad she'd put a noose around her own neck.

That thought brought Mr. Famous back to Claire. She, too, loved attention but claimed she sought it out for a very pragmatic reason. Her philosophy was that you had to be a name brand. It made good business sense. She declared this as if she were quoting from the Wharton Business School scriptures. The implication was that only someone unsophisticated and uneducated would think it was about anything else. She was very convincing, but lately he'd been wondering if Claire's arrogance was just better bullshit, fancier camouflage. Maybe her noose was hidden under an Hermès scarf.

He bench-pressed another set. On the last rep, he could

feel the pain ripping through his muscles. This was the part he loved and hated the most. The burn hurt like hell but it was the only way to build strength. And just when he got to the place where he didn't think he could hold the position another second, the TV reporter segued into an item about The Rock's movie breaking box office records. He forced himself to hold for another count of ten. And then another five as a private fuck-you to his competition.

twelve

s I lay in bed that first night in Falmouth, I rehearsed what I was going to say to Mr. F in the morning. I refined it down to this one sentence: "Uh, I'm a little confused about my job responsibilities since we're staying at an inn."

When the plan was set, back in California, I'd assumed we'd be staying in a house. My exact assumption was a house near the water. Scenic view. I wasn't imagining Malibu East, but I definitely didn't expect this quaint destination. Movie star and quaint destination didn't seem to go together. And what exactly was I supposed to be doing if I wasn't cooking? Was I invited along as a traveling companion? And if so, why didn't Mr. F just come out and tell me that? Could it be because that sounded too pathetic, as if he were paying someone to be his friend? Or maybe he didn't think about it at all. A person having a breakdown (or a "free fall," as he called it) is not required to be logical. Or even truthful.

I considered just going along with it. That would be the smart thing to do. The interesting thing. To see what evolves without trying to define it could even be healthy. But I'm not good at not knowing who I am to someone I'm traveling with. I needed to know what box I was in. Chances are I'd be jumping out of that box in a minute but not knowing the point of origin was unsettling.

So unsettling that at midnight, I went downstairs to the quaint lobby, where I found only one person on the job—a man wearing an L.L. Bean flannel jacket. He looked more like a handyman and I doubted he had ever heard the word "concierge," but he was the guy in charge.

"Is there a neighborhood bar you could recommend?"

"Well, there are . . . " He stopped. "You mean now?" He looked at the clock. "At five after midnight?"

"Is that too late?"

"Off season it is. Unless you want to drive back down the highway. About three miles. Jerry's Roadside. They get a late crowd."

"What kind of crowd?" Not that I could be choosy. But if it was some biker bar or something out of *The Accused* I'd go back to my room, pop an Ambien, go to sleep and hopefully do some more California dreaming.

"On weekends kids drive up from SMU."

I assumed that was a college, though the only SMU I'd ever heard of was in the South. "And it's how many miles?"

"About three."

"You got a number for a taxi service?"

"Don't want to drink and drive. That's smart."

"I'm not a big drinker but since I don't have a car maybe

I will tonight. Maybe I'll just tear up the town." Something made me want to jolt his New England complacency. Clearly I failed because he looked like he was hardly breathing.

"Your car's right there," he said.

"What?"

He pointed out the window. "Tony's Rent-a-Car delivered it a few hours ago."

It was a Cadillac. New. Convertible. Definitely not your typical Hertz rental. Definitely not your typical Cadillac.

"All the way from New Bedford," the old man added. "I left a message for your boss."

"Lilac? He rented a lilac Cadillac?"

He handed me the keys. "I don't know what you asked for, but looks like this is what you got."

Jerry's Roadside was still open and still lively. The place was about half full, with most of the action at the tables along the wall. At first glance, the crowd seemed to be comprised solely of old geezers and locals and I felt like an extra in the bar scene in *The Perfect Storm*. Where were the SMU coeds? Talk about feeling out of place. Was it my imagination or did a couple of the locals eye me suspiciously, as if I were an interloper, someone who had wandered in from another movie.

I took a seat at the vacant end of the bar and ordered a glass of white wine. "No, wait, let me change that," I said to the bartender, who, oddly enough, bore a resemblance to Mark Wahlberg. "Make that a vodka soda. You got Ketel One?"

"We got Absolut. We got Stoli." He could tell by my expression that I wasn't excited by the choices. "If you want more fire, Jerry keeps a couple of bottles of Polish vodka in the back. Ten bucks a shot but two sips will knock you on your ass."

"Absolut will be fine," I said. "And lots of lemon."

"That'll be extra," he said.

"Fine."

"I'm kidding." He smiled. "Christ, you L.A. people."

What? How did he know I was from L.A.? It's not as if I'd walked in there wearing sunglasses and Juicy Couture sweats, though I did have both in my suitcase.

"You're all into that Ketel One stuff." He shot a look over to a corner table, which wasn't visible from the front door. A half dozen people, who were definitely not locals, were partying hard. They certainly looked like they could be from L.A. Movie business L.A.

One guy, who seemed the leader of the group (his two buddies hung on his every word) had a style I call upscale scruffy. Expensive but messy haircut and a frayed T-shirt that said NOT EVERYONE CAN HANDLE THE FRUIT ON THE VINE. Across from him a girl was searching through her Prada ponyskin bag till she found her compact. Even from the bar I recognized the silver case. T. LeClerc powder—made in France, sold at Barney's. While checking out her face she continued to carry on a conversation with a woman who was dancing next to her table—dancing alone, or with the whole bar, depending on how you wanted to look at it. Everything about her was a cry for attention. The way she moved and definitely the way she was dressed. Low-rise pants, and I mean low, with a pack of Marlboro Lights tucked inside the waistband. Even more provocative was her sheer top, the kind that only really works on a nineteen-year-old model strutting down a runway. This woman was probably in her thirties and the seven hundred dollars she paid for that Stella McCartney top (I saw it on the second floor at Neiman's) would have been better spent on a shrink. Dr. Davenport has some interesting things to say about obsessive attention disorder—my name for it. His theory being that most disorders in Hollywood stem from too much or too little attention. The dancer performing for the whole room obviously couldn't get enough. But she did succeed in keeping my focus, which was why I didn't notice the third girl in the group until she screamed.

"Oh my God!"

I threw an "Oh my God!" right back at her. I knew Elizabeth West was working on a movie—rewriting somewhere on location—but I never expected to run into her or anyone else I knew in this bar. She climbed over the girl with the compact to run over and give me a hug. "What are *you* doing *here*?"

"I'm here working," I said. "Well, sort of."

"I love sort of. Sort of is always interesting."

The bartender placed my drink down on the bar.

"Add it to my tab," Elizabeth said. Ignoring her friends, she settled into the seat next to mine. "Working for who?" she asked.

"For Mr. F."

"Mr. F is here?"

"At an inn, a few miles up the road."

Now she looked back at the girl who was dancing. "Uh-oh," she said. She then helped herself to a big sip of my drink and said it again. "Uh-oh." But this time she cracked a smile.

Elizabeth and I are the kind of friends who can go without seeing each other for months and then pick up immediately where we left off. People say we talk alike and think alike but I could never do what she does. Writing spec screenplays in Hollywood these days has got to be one of the most frustrating ways to make a living, especially for someone like Elizabeth, who likes to write complex stories with a lot of ambiguity. Studios don't like to make movies that crosswire good and bad unless it's done as some kind of Halloween fright flick, but Elizabeth keeps writing them anyway. Last year she published a collection of short stories entitled *Anyway*, all about people who know the odds are against them but choose to continue doing whatever it is they're doing. It didn't get a lot of publicity (not a flashy enough concept) but managed to get a buzz going on the Internet—*anyway*.

Though her books and message movies don't earn her serious bucks in Hollywood, her attitude is a bigger problem. She doesn't play the game the way it's supposed to be played and people find it unnerving. I once saw her go up to an influential gossip columnist who had trashed a number of Hollywood celebrities who opposed the war in Iraq. In a detached way, as if she were a sociologist reporting on the behavioral patterns of some primitive culture, she asked the reporter if he would have been so opinionated if his boss wasn't a right-wing war zealot.

Weeks later the journalist retaliated by trashing her book and making nasty innuendos about Elizabeth and her "so-called relationship with a certain married director." If he thought he was going to get to her, he was so wrong. She shrugged it off. "I drew blood first," she said.

Oh, and just so you don't hate my friend Elizabeth, thinking she's one of *those* women, Elizabeth was with Jake, the director, before he was married. The bigger question here is not why she still sees him but why did Jake's wife marry him knowing he sees other women? Or maybe no questions are required. More and more relationships in Hollywood are treated the way gays are in the military. The proper etiquette is, don't ask, don't tell.

Elizabeth and I were having our own little party at the bar with frequent visits from the dancing girl, whose name was Layla. She was one of those generic blondes, pretty enough but no stand-out. And maybe because of that, she made a big effort to snag attention by flaunting her taut, tanned body. She'd twirl over our way and move seductively in front of us. Then abruptly she'd turn her back on us and dance for the guy with the frayed T-shirt. Elizabeth filled me in. The guy, Jonas, was the cinematographer on the movie they were shooting—a low-budget production with some artsy elements (including Jonas, the script, and a great production designer). Layla, who Elizabeth described as a second-rate Linda Fiorentino, had a supporting role. The "uh-oh" comment was because Layla and the cinematographer were sort of seeing each other, but if Layla knew Mr. F was in town—alone—she'd show up at his door in the middle of the night. She was always in search of a bigger headline, and whether she really deep down believed she was irresistible or was just faking it till she made it, the end result was the same. Knock. Knock.

I chased my first drink with a shot of the Polish vodka. A second after it went down my throat, my story and my confusion came pouring out.

"Do you think Mr. F just wanted company for the trip? Maybe my job is to feed him in other ways. Feed his ego. Feed his spirit."

"That's always your job," Elizabeth answered, who in spite of her intake of alcohol managed to sound as clear and concise as Dr. Davenport. "It's the job of every employee. But," she added, "I wouldn't rule out the chef role entirely. Look, he's a celebrity. More than that—he's a celebrity who grew up around here. He's their boy. Let me tell you how it could have gone down. The owner of the inn gets a call from the only hometown boy who ever made it in Hollywood. The owner is probably so thrilled he's talking to the big movie star he'd go along with any special requests. So when Mr. F. says, Look, the thing is I'm on a special diet and I'll be bringing my chef with me. Any problem with her using your kitchen to prepare meals? What do you think the owner of the inn is going to say? He's not going to check with his staff. He's not worried about it totally fucking with the routine of the kitchen to have someone's private chef in there. He's talking to the town's only local hero. He's talking to the biggest celebrity guest the inn has ever had. He's talking to someone who for all he knows may have fucked Julia Roberts. He's going to say yes. No problem. Whatever you need."

Listening to her, it all made so much sense that I felt silly that I'd considered anything but that scenario. I also have to admit I felt a little disappointed. I was beginning to like the idea that I was invited along for my company, not my egg white and tomato omelette.

Elizabeth picked up on my little mood. "I'm not saying he didn't have other reasons for inviting you along, I'm just saying right now those other reasons are between him and him."

When the phone rang at three A.M., waking me out of a half hour of sleep, I wasn't worried. The boss's free fall did not abide by any clock.

"I think we should go back to you calling me Victor," he said. The structure of that sentence struck me—"we," as if it were a joint effort.

He'd always seemed to enjoy my playful nickname for him, but maybe it was the last thing he wanted to be called now that he felt his fame slipping away.

"Victor? Not Vic?" I teased.

"Let's stick with Victor, okay?"

"Okay."

"Good night, Luce," he said sweetly and hung up.

Luce? He was losing a nickname and I was gaining one? Not even Lucy. But Luce. I was tempted to call back and say I think we should go back to you calling me Lucinda. But I didn't because the fact is he was the only one in the world who'd ever called me Luce and I kind of liked it. And when I thought about it for a second, I decided wanting to be called Victor might be a good sign. Maybe it was all part of his efforts to reclaim his real self. Maybe Dr. Davenport's words had gotten through. I was imagining a rapid road to recovery when the phone rang again.

"Hello, Victor," I said.

He was now laughing maniacally. "I forgot to ask. What do you think of that lilac Cadillac?"

Okay, maybe not so rapid.

thirteen

T he staff in the kitchen stared at me as if I were a
freak. They had reason to. The vodka from the night
before showed up in dark circles under my eyes,
which I hid by wearing violet-lens glasses. It wasn't because
I was trying to look cool, it was because I couldn't stand to
look at my reflection in the mirror that hung on a wall next
to the chopping block. It caught natural light from a side
window as well as a fluorescent overhead. A deadly combination. Whoever hung that mirror there must hate women.
I doubt that any female over twenty-eight didn't shudder at
her reflection. And if she didn't, it was probably a sign of
resignation, not emotional maturity. I was also sporting a
cockeyed ponytail, which was held in place by a bright orange hair ornament. Violet lenses and orange ornaments.
Not exactly New England colors.

Even if I were in blues and grays they would have stared
at me because I was scrambling eggs for a movie star. They
watched me prepare a room service tray for him as if they
were observing a religious rite. I'd been in the world of

celebrities long enough to recognize what was going on. Knowing details of a star's life—that they liked their scrambled eggs well done and cooked with tomatoes and just a sliver of onion—made fans feel closer to their idol. Entertainment magazines and "news" shows banked on this kind of fan curiosity. If we were in L.A., someone in the kitchen crew might phone the item in (albeit somewhat embellished) to a tabloid and make a quick fifty bucks. But in this small Cape Cod town, a hometown celebrity was to be protected, not exploited. Or maybe I'm just romanticizing quaintness.

Victor was watching TV with the sound off when I brought in his breakfast. I forced myself to think of him as Victor now, and I have to say it wasn't that hard to get used to. Maybe that's because name changes are not uncommon in L.A. In the last year alone, three people I know have adopted new names on the advice of their spiritual master.

"News anchors have the most annoying voices," he said without looking up.

He hit the off button on the remote and remained sitting on the couch, which in daylight looked more shabby than homey. In fact everything about the place was subpar, especially for a star who considered the Four Seasons second rate. The inn's idea of style was to hang decorative plates on the wall, plates that rattled whenever the people upstairs walked across their room.

"*Bon appétit*," I said, a little too cheery, but I figured fake frivolity was better than no frivolity at all.

I placed the tray on the coffee table. Victor immediately picked up his fork and started eating, though without any sign of enjoyment. He was robotic in his movements and his eyes seemed dazed and unfocused. They didn't move or appear to blink, even when his upstairs neighbor dropped something that sounded like a heavy suitcase, causing more rattling here below.

"Who hangs plates like paintings?" I waited for a response but got none. "They're *plates*," I continued. "That's breakable china up there. I don't get it. If plates, why not forks? Knives? A case could be made that certain silverware styles are just as decorative as any plate."

Usually my wacky observations would inspire some kind of remark. When in a good mood, Victor could respond with a fifteen-minute rebuttal that was equally wacky. That day—nothing. I would have given anything for a burst of last night's maniacal laughter.

I considered leaving, going back to my room, but he was starting to worry me. And for purely selfish reasons I didn't want to worry. I wanted him to say or do something to assure me that he was okay so I could go back to my room and not think about him for a minute. I also wanted to make sure he had everything he needed so I could wash my hair and give my face a mud mask without being summoned mid-maintenance and having to rinse off prematurely and return to refill his coffee.

It was only when he finished his breakfast that he spoke. "I hate this place."

"Not the way you remembered it?"

He stuck the garnish—a sprig of parsley—in his mouth and chewed on the end of it as if there were something to chew. I waited for more of a response but, again, got none.

"Any thoughts on lunch?" It was a ridiculous question,

seeing as he'd just had his last bite of breakfast and was paying me to think about lunch so he didn't have to.

He took the wilting sprig out of his mouth and tossed it
down on his empty plate.

"Cut," I said as if he were doing a scene and I was the
director. I don't know where that came from. I shocked myself as much as I shocked him. But it worked. He stood up;
he was ready to move on.

"We're going out," he said.

"Out where?"

"Wherever the lilac Cadillac wants to take us."

He lied. He had a destination. He cruised through the
streets of his old neighborhood, block after block of
small wooden houses with tiny front yards. One yard had a
statue of the Virgin Mary out front, another had a jungle
gym and a third had a lot of weeds. Faith, kids and poverty.
It kind of summed up the area. At least the sun was out and
occasionally we'd drive by a blast of color. A house painted
pink. Another painted St. Patrick's Day green. That put a
smile on my face, not Mr. F's. Oops, I mean Victor's.

Eventually, he started talking. "Used to be a store right
here," he said, pointing to a dry cleaners on the corner.
"Groceries in the front and pinball machines in the back.
Duke was the name of the guy who ran the place. That
back room was his office. Walls were covered with pic-
tures of naked girls. Some from magazines. Some Duke
had taken himself, which is a scary thing if you knew
Duke. The guy was sixty, looked eighty, and had the sex
drive of a twenty-year-old. His idea of hot was like some-

thing from an R. Crumb comic. He liked weight. Big thighs. Monster tits."

As Victor drove up and down these streets, circling some blocks over and over again, he filled me in on what it was like to be a sixteen-year-old, hanging with the most fucked-up kids in town. I couldn't decide if it was a good sign that he was talking again or a bad sign that he was talking about the kind of depressing scenarios that are not helped by retrospect. I was losing my ability to identify sanity. Was it healthy to see one's past realistically? Or was it unhealthy to dwell on it? It was a question I never contemplated when in Hollywood because most people there have told so many lies about their past, reality was not an option. It was like those women in their fifties who have been coloring their hair since they were teenagers. Try asking them what their natural color is. At best, you'll get an honest guess. And they certainly won't dwell on it because they're too busy fantasizing their future.

"I'm missing L.A.," I announced, though it had nothing to do with anything Victor was talking about. "I miss the land of a million dreams."

He looked at me as if he couldn't believe he was stuck in a car with someone who talked like that. "Land of a million dreams? What are you, nuts?"

"Sorry. I don't know where that came from. It's like a line from the worst poem ever written."

"I don't care where it's from. There aren't a million dreams in L.A. Only one. BE A STAR."

Then he broke into his maniacal laugh and turned the Cadillac down a new street.

. . .

Who knew that that turn would change everything? At first all I noticed was a small playground. When Victor parked the car, I saw that there was a basketball court occupied by about ten or so kids tossing a ball around.

"This was my home," Victor said as he got out of the car. He was walking four or five steps ahead of me, blocking a clear view of the court. I had no idea why he stopped abruptly. I almost collided with him because I was thinking about a shower and my new facial scrub back at the inn. It was impossible for me to feel good about anything when I had stringy hair and clogged pores.

"What's wrong?" I asked.

He ignored me and moved over to a hilly spot, which provided a better view of the on-court action. He was beginning to piss me off. I was tempted to wait in the car but that felt like something a pouty girlfriend would do, not an employee. So I rejoined him and the second I did he moved again—this time to about fifteen yards behind the basket. I felt like an idiot following him. Suddenly it all felt so sexist and misogynistic and I never think like that. If he would at least answer my question, I could go back to chalking up his behavior to simply crazy and unaware. I was about to turn bitchy until I got right up in his face and it became clear that something was very, very wrong. He had tears in his eyes and he wasn't acting. I know this because he's never been able to cry in any of his movies. At most he gets a far-away look that's meant to suggest that even though he's just saved the world, he's more than a superhero. He's human and pained by the human condition. This show of faux emotion was always helped by a dramatic soundtrack. But these tears were real and there was no soulful piano piece to help them along. I wondered what the fuck was going on. I knew Victor wasn't overcome with nostalgia over his childhood playground. This wasn't a Madonna song.

I followed his gaze, which was locked on that basketball court. Among the players was a kid I hadn't noticed before, maybe because he'd been on the sidelines. But now he was right in the middle of the action and hard to miss because he was the only one in a wheelchair. Have to add, he had an awesome bank shot (left-handed off the glass) as well as pretty impressive mobility in that two-wheeler. The kid could even play defense. Victor watched transfixed as if the whole scene were a visit from the ghost of Christmas past. In a way it was. I thought he must be thinking of Ned, his younger brother, who'd died years before. Isabel was the one who'd told me about Ned, the invalid sibling, in the course of lecturing me on the benefits of calcium and kelp.

Victor watched the kid take a few shots and score another two points. When it went through the basket, hitting nothing but net, Victor clenched his fist like a coach proud of his rookie. For another twenty minutes we followed the game in progress, until the break, when the kid in the wheelchair was pushed up a ramp and into the back of his buddy's van. It was only after they were completely gone from sight that Victor sat on the ground, his head in his hands, and sobbed.

I didn't know what to do. I'm not good with women getting emotional, much less men. As I said, I have a little problem with emotional intimacy. Dr. Davenport says it's no accident that I ended up working for a man whose on-screen image is all about toughness and autonomy. But that was not the man in front of me now, and I knew I should attempt to do something to comfort him. A better woman would be able to offer solace with a hug. I contemplated holding his hand and saying, "Look, I know what you're going through [even though I didn't really] and it's going to be all right." Saying it's going to be all right was important, I decided. So I inched my way closer and awkwardly put my hand on his shoulder and said it, but not too convincingly. For all I knew my hand on Victor's shoulder was more annoying than comforting. Still, I kept it there, because I was afraid that if I removed it, I'd go into a decline over my inability to connect when connection wasn't just an option, but an obligation that came with being part of the human race. And then I realized that even thinking that, though very human, was inhumane. It was narcissistic to be thinking about how this pertained to me. There was a crying man to deal with. I took a mini step closer and grabbed his shoulder a little tighter. We stayed in that strange pose until Victor broke the contact by standing up.

"Increments," he said.

"Increments?"

"It changes in increments."

I didn't press him for an explanation, but as we got back into the Caddie, I tried to recall the exact definition of the word "increment." A small step? A small portion?

And while I was thinking small, Victor went big.

"I want to get back to L.A. as soon as possible. Today. Now."

I could have gone through a list of reasons why that

would be difficult. To start—time, distance and rush-hour traffic. I pictured us missing the plane at Logan and Victor blaming me. Celebrities are used to having producers, producer's assistants and dozens of people on the set to make things happen. Logistics are always to be worked out by other people. They've done their part. They gave the order. I've learned through working for my boss that explaining the complications involved in one of his requests only leads to frustration on his part and insecurity on mine. (He could replace me with someone who can actually find a way to make a fat-free/healthy chocolate cake that tastes as good as the one his mother used to make from a mix.) I learned to offer two options. One that he'd hate. And one that was actually do-able.

"Okay," I said. "We can try to charter a plane for, what? Fifty thousand dollars? Or we can fly out first thing tomorrow. Whatever you want. I'll make all the arrangements."

I knew nothing about chartering planes but I was betting on the fact that he wouldn't want to spend $50,000 for a ride home. I also knew he didn't want it to look as if money was the issue. He had just had a cathartic emotional moment. Money shouldn't matter. It never did for movie heroes.

"Though," I added sweetly, "you might not be happy with what's available. On short notice, you often get stuck with a tiny six-seater. Plus," I added, "the weather out of Logan could be a problem." Not that I knew what the forecast was, but even action heroes have to make adjustments for Mother Nature.

I could tell he was wavering so I pressed for a decision.

"But I'll arrange it if you want or we could go back tomorrow morning."

"Bad weather? Huh. Well, no point in . . ." He sighed instead of finishing his sentence. Resigned, he turned to me and said, "What will we do tonight?"

Somehow my chef job had morphed into being his assistant and his party planner. I didn't mind. Finally he'd asked a question I knew how to answer. I may have a long way to go before becoming a "better woman," but I knew a thing or two about being a fun girl.

fourteen

Sex was in the air. Even if it wasn't, I would have encouraged Victor in that direction because I believe the only real upside to one's life falling apart is that often the sex gets better. I base this theory on my own experience with an across-the-board collapse. Five years before, in the space of three months, I lost my job, broke up with my boyfriend, ran out of money, had to move into a friend's tiny guest bedroom and woke one morning to see that the doors had been stolen off my uninsured Jeep. It felt biblical.

But assuming one can get out of the fetal position and hook up with someone, sex during a collapse can be extraordinary because you are completely in the moment. You don't want to dwell on the past because how great could it have been if it brought you to the point where it takes everything you've got to pick yourself up off the floor. Dwelling on the future is worse, unless you're the type who thinks adversity builds character. My experience is that ad-

versity builds resentment and results in a bad diet of Coke,
chips and salsa. Being in the moment is the only upside to
being down.

We got to Jerry's Roadside at nine-thirty. I'd called Elizabeth West earlier and begged her to show up with
her friends. Otherwise it was just going to be Victor and me
drinking Polish vodka and trying not to cross any lines that
would result in my waking up the next morning wondering if I was out of my mind or out of a job.

Elizabeth was there when we arrived, along with about
half a dozen of her movie pals. They were at the same table
they'd camped out at the other night, eating some of Jerry's
finest specialties: grilled cheese sandwiches, curly fries and
chicken chili. I waved to them before settling into a nearby
booth with my boss. Elizabeth got up and came over to chat.
That was the correct protocol. Victor was a movie star. He
didn't need to join anyone else's party. That's not how it
worked unless he was in the mood to work it that way.
Everybody knew the deal. You pay your respects to the big
guy and move on. Elizabeth would have said a quick hello
and goodbye had not Layla, the dancing girl from the other
night, struck a pose at our table. She was wearing a T-shirt
that said BITE ME. I was so over people talking with their
clothes.

"I'm exhausted," she said as if we all knew who she was
and might be interested in the level of her fatigue.

Elizabeth made the introductions.

Layla turned to Victor. "So, here we are in Cape Cod."

An uninformed person would think the two had actually met before. They hadn't but Layla was assuming the privileges that come from being a club member. Elizabeth didn't have to explain that one to me. It's a common practice in Hollywood. Plenty of people believe that if you have any degree of fame, you're allowed to engage any other famous person in conversation, provided they're not in the middle of shooting or fucking. Now Victor may have seen Layla in some movie or TV show, but working for scale plus ten percent does not put you in Victor's ten-million-(and shrinking)-per-picture category. And even if he was on a downward spiral and might never see that kind of paycheck again, he had once commanded top billing and top dollar. The fact that Layla didn't seem to get that and because she nudged Elizabeth aside to get to Victor's side of the table brought out my hostility.

"Let me ask you something. What would you do if someone actually bit you, right here, right now?"

"What?"

"Your shirt," I explained.

She glanced down at her ample chest and laughed. "Oh, is that what it says? I always forget what I'm wearing."

Who always forgets what they're wearing? There was no chance of this being true, which didn't bother Layla in the least. I was beginning to notice a new trend with certain young L.A. girls. Lying blatantly was in, as was a whole new code. There was a tacit agreement not to bust each other on anything. Words and deeds need not have a correlation. Entertain, don't explain, was the new motto, which I suppose is a legitimate approach, assuming you know how to entertain.

Layla looked over to the table where Jonas, her cinematographer and sometime boyfriend, was sitting, scowling.

"Am I not allowed to talk to people anymore? He's driving me crazy." It was her way of bragging. Anyone could read between those lines to get her real message: He is so possessive of me because I'm so hot.

Seeing an opportunity to escape, Elizabeth took it. "I'll calm him down," she said, leaving Layla with two people who didn't know about her romantic history and didn't care.

Layla fixed her attention on Victor.

"But I can't piss him off too much, can I? He'll light me from a bad angle tomorrow and it's my big scene."

If she hadn't said "my big scene," I might have shut up. Instead I blurted out the kind of thing I'd say if I'd spent the whole night drinking Jerry's back-room vodka.

"Well, what'll it be? Victor or your career?"

My boss laughed, and then talking out of the corner of his mouth like he did when he played the gangster in *Streetwise,* he said, "I'd say you've got about another minute before your guy decides for you."

Layla watched Jonas throw down some cash for the check and grab his jacket.

"I'm not good with either/or situations," she announced, as if that gave her the moral edge. She got up and went over to sit at the bar by herself.

She was pulling the kind of move that I'd seen countless times before from an assortment of manipulative L.A. women. First Layla set up the expectation that she was going to be fun and flirty and then abruptly withheld all attention and affection. Played out on a grand scale it meant she could go from sitting on your lap to slapping your face.

Unfortunately, this switch hitting often works. Although Victor did look stunned and a little hurt, he also seemed a little more intrigued.

"You want me to translate that flirt-and-run for you?" I asked.

"I get it," he said. "I just don't have the energy for it."

And yet he kept looking at Layla as she sipped her vodka soda at the bar. Yeah, right, I thought. He doesn't have the energy not to go for it.

No one left. Not even Jonas. After a while he even looked like he was enjoying himself, ordering more drinks and talking mostly to Elizabeth and occasionally to someone from his crew. It was a case of Hollywood people only mingling with other Hollywood people. There we all were three thousand miles from home and no one seemed to have the slightest curiosity about the locals. Not even Victor, who had come all this way to reconnect with his roots. In spite of his protests, he kept his focus on Layla, who abruptly returned to our table and continued her flirting as if she'd never stopped. I decided to make it easy for both of them and left them alone so they could accelerate the inevitable. Female fame chaser meets male movie star action hero who needs a little lust and attention. What were the odds those two weren't destined to share a bed?

I joined Elizabeth, who immediately got up as if she were saving my seat.

"Got to go," she said.

Jonas looked at her askance, as if to say you've got to be kidding. I did say it, and then pulled her aside.

"Why are you leaving? It's not late."

"Jonas is working his way through a bottle of tequila and he's looking to make Layla jealous. As smart and interesting as the guy is, that's not for me."

"He's also very cute," I pointed out.

"I guess," Elizabeth replied as she pulled her car keys out of her pocket. "But you know me, I'm not interested in anyone other than Jake."

I did know her and knew she was a one-man woman in love with a multi-women man. "I keep expecting that to change," I said.

"I don't rule it out but I've yet to meet a man who can top Jake."

Was she in love? In obsession? In denial?

She must have picked up on my silent musings because she laughed. "I have been described as a volunteer prisoner."

She kissed me on the cheek. "Don't you rule it out," she added, giving me a friendly push in Jonas's direction before heading out the door.

I sat down next to the cute cinematographer, who did not look as if that seat next to him had my name on it.

"You mind?" I asked.

He took a moment to answer, as if I'd asked a deeply personal question, one that possibly bordered on impolite. Finally he spoke. "Swell" he said.

"Is that swell as in no problem? Swell as in could be interesting? Or swell as in my life sucks and this is further proof of my bad luck?"

He took another gulp of his drink. "Could you stick to true or false questions? I don't have the energy for this."

It was becoming the theme of the night. Having energy. Not having energy. Which brought me back around to Victor and Layla. I looked over to see how their little hookup was going. I guess it was going real swell because they were gone.

"He left? I can't fucking believe he left!" I stood up and looked over to the now vacant table, where a waitress was clearing off the glasses. "He left without telling me?" The questions weren't directed at anyone in particular, but Jonas replied, "What are you so mad about? He left with my girlfriend."

He had a point and I have to say he was taking it pretty well, no doubt helped by the tequila. I sat back down.

"But we drove here together. What am I supposed to do now?" Even as I said this it occurred to me I could call a taxi. No big deal. It wasn't really the transportation issue that upset me. It was the fact that my boss didn't bother to say anything. Was I so insignificant that I didn't rate a goodbye? I would have been content with something as simple as "See you back at the inn." Or, "Are you going to be okay on your own?"

"Maybe he's coming back," Jonas said. "Could be he and Layla will just do a quick cruise around the block." He managed to keep a very even tone and at the same time communicate that he now considered Layla a skanky whore. Nonchalant bitterness was a style that became him.

"Come on, I'll give you a lift," he said.

"You've got a car?"

"No."

"So how are you going to give me a lift?"

"I'll steal one."

. . .

He didn't have to. Not that he was the stealing kind. I'd never met a cinematographer who wasn't more poet than felon. Circumstances prevented him from proving me wrong, because much to my surprise, the lilac Cadillac was outside where we'd parked it. The keys were in the ignition.

"What the . . . ?"

"Layla's car is gone," Jonas said.

"Oh." For a second I felt relieved. I wasn't so insignificant that I'd been deserted without an explanation or a ride. But now what? What did this mean? Was I supposed to wait here in case Victor returned? Or should I drive myself back to the inn, assuming that's what my boss intended?

"He could have left a note."

"If he didn't want to stop to say good night, why would he want to stop, find a pen and a piece of paper and write you a note?" As Jonas talked he opened the passenger side of the Caddie and got in. Under the bright light in the parking lot, he looked older than I first thought. Late thirties with the kind of lanky, angular body that would look good with an electric guitar in his hands.

"Am I giving you a ride home?" I asked, not that I minded.

"No, you're driving us both back to your place and we're going to shag for hours." His sudden adoption of a British accent and Brit lingo made me laugh, which, I believe, was his intention. Not that he'd say no if I agreed to go along with some bonking.

"I don't think so," I said.

"Don't think," he replied. "Thinking is for pussies."

I didn't stop thinking but I did use my brain to justify bringing Jonas back to my room. Why not? To begin with, all night I'd felt that sex was in the air. The moon looked a day away from full and the air had a crispness to it that put me in a very "seize the moment" mood. And though my life wasn't in a deep collapse, it was teetering on one, which made sex with a cute cinematographer seem like a good short-term remedy. Or maybe no sex. Maybe companionship and a little snogging was all I needed. Why is it, I wondered, as I exited off the highway ramp, that British words for kissing and fucking are so cute? Between their cutesy vocabulary and a proper accent even the skankiest behavior can come across as innocent and respectable. I decided I was going to proceed in a British state of mind—at least for the rest of the evening. Except in one area. My American common sense inspired me to insist on one condition. I vetoed Jonas's suggestion that we stop and pick up more tequila. I was all for getting a little wild but not so wild that I wouldn't be able to get out of bed in the morning. I had a plane to catch. I had sunny L.A. on the other end of that ride. And I had a boss who was probably going to be so hungover, I'd have to nurse his headache while navigating our way out to Logan.

"Rules." Jonas smiled. "Already we got rules." But he dropped the subject after that and leaned over and licked my face. It could have been sloppy and disgusting but it was actually erotic. I increased the speed up to fifty in a thirty-five-MPH zone. I was being cautiously wild. The thought did occur to me that since my room was just two doors down from Victor's, it was possible Jonas and Layla could cross paths in the hallway. It wasn't the best-case scenario but then again it wasn't the worst. And if it happened, well, maybe we could all wish each other lots of love and part with a "big kiss, darling," just like Brits do. It was a fantasy, of course, because the truth was none of us were British. We were all so American, which meant that we would proceed confidently and then be totally shocked when things didn't work out the way we'd planned.

My room may have been two doors away from Victor's but he got the corner spot—a suite with a view. I got one room with half a view. The building next door cut into my scenery but I didn't care. I had low expectations when it came to accommodations—and apparently men. I didn't expect Jonas to put much energy into seducing me. I didn't expect any declarations of attraction. I didn't expect him to pretend he'd wanted me from "hello." However, I also didn't expect that he would start things off with a disclaimer. We'd hardly gotten our coats off, hardly gotten acquainted, though we were on a fast track. As soon as we got inside the room, Jonas pulled out a pack of cigarettes. "You want one?"

"Nope."

He hesitated before lighting up. "You hate this?"

"Not at all. I'm a big fan of secondhand smoke."

In that case, he grabbed me and kissed me, a nice long kiss that left us both smiling. And that's when he came out with it.

"Just so you know, I'm not looking for anything complicated."

He might as well have said you're just filler. That's the

nerve it hit in me, maybe because a lot of men don't understand the difference between separate issue and filler, and I've had the misfortune to meet a number of them. I didn't mind being a separate issue, separate from Jonas's involvement with Layla. Separate from his life back in L.A. Separate from his fantasy of the perfect girl. But I was not interested in just filling the vacuum created by the end of one relationship and the start of a good night's sleep. I found it insulting. Making this situation even worse was that guys usually fuck you first and then come up with the disclaimer. That may be more deceitful, but at least it tells you they really want to fuck you. Leading with a disclaimer meant Jonas was willing to jeopardize potential sex, which meant he wasn't all that into me to begin with. Whichever way I looked at it, it was crushing to my dwindling self-esteem.

"Not looking for anything complicated?" My happy smile was replaced by my sarcastic smile. Thinner lips, wider grin. "Really, and I thought you were shopping for a profound committed connection."

I reached over and grabbed the cigarette out of his hand and settled into an armchair, which was upholstered in quaint floral flannel. My body language said I'm not moving and you shouldn't bother making a trip across the room to apologize.

"See! See! This is what I'm trying to avoid. This!" He walked toward me but then stopped midway.

"This?" I exhaled.

"Yes. This. You and me arguing about something before there's anything to argue about."

"If I understood you correctly, your point was you weren't looking for this to be anything."

"I meant, let's not let the sex confuse stuff."

"There is no sex. There's been some kissing. There's been some talking. Some smoking. But no sex. Not happening."

"Fine with me." He sat on the floral upholstered couch. "But can we keep the kissing, smoking, talking thing going?"

"No, yes and yes."

An hour later, the distance between us had narrowed but we were still more than an arm's length apart. Both of us were sitting on the floor. There had been no kissing, a minimum amount of smoking and lots and lots of talking. Most of it erotic meanderings. We started off making general statements about why sex confuses things between men and women and very quickly moved on to confessing the specific things that got us hot. Sexy stories at arm's length can be very arousing. Very. It was hard to avoid noticing the tent pole inside Jonas's jeans. The bulge made me smile, an affirmation of my storytelling and hopefully the glimpse of cleavage I was flashing.

"Want to see it?" he asked.

"Are you one of those guys who has to show it?"

"Some girls like to look."

"I'm mildly curious."

He reached for his zipper.

"But . . ."

He stopped. "What?"

"You have to keep your distance. There can't be any touching between you and me."

"Oh, the no touching game. What are we, fifteen?"

"Did you do this at fifteen?"

"Maybe."

"What else did you do?"

"Else? I didn't say I did this."

"But you didn't say you didn't."

Some guys have such beautiful equipment I get penis envy just looking at it. I once dated a man who had made a lot of money creating successful television shows. He was considered a very eligible desirable bachelor. It was considered a big deal to be invited over to his house to view his art collection—including a very famous Magritte over his bed. I made it over to his place a few times, but I couldn't tell you a thing about that Magritte, or any of his other treasures, because he happened to be one of those guys with a dick that could have inspired Michelangelo. It never even occurred to me to check out the paintings on his wall because, as far as I was concerned, he was the work of art.

Now Jonas wasn't quite in that league but he was close, so I kept the sex talk going and this time it did lead to touching. Jonas honored our agreement but at my encouragement he started touching himself. I became a spectator, and a verbal participant. My words were the equivalent of strokes. A part of me felt like a teenager. There was something so innocent about this game. And so safe. I revealed nothing. I remained buttoned and zipped. A proper, good girl, with the mind of a slut. I thought about sucking my finger, to further enhance the mood, but it seemed too elementary and, besides, Jonas didn't need any extra stimulation. I have to admit there was an element of revenge in my pleasure. It was a way of saying you may not think of me as girlfriend material, but I don't consider you lover mate-

rial. Not even one-night-stand material. We're show-and-
tell pals. That's all. You show and I tell.

When he finally came, I handed him some Kleenex and
a cigarette. "Well, that was fun," I said, feeling strangely
powerful. So powerful I felt no need to stay on my side of
the great invisible divide.

"Glad you enjoyed it," he said as he pulled himself
together.

I put my hand on his arm, to let him know the no touching rule was no longer in effect.

"I should be going," he said, looking a little sheepish.

"Can't believe it's after two o'clock already," I said as I
walked him to the door. I fully expected another kiss that
would once again leave us both smiling.

"Uh . . . you're really something," he said.

"So are you."

He took out his lighter and lit up another cigarette. He
took a deep drag and blew out the smoke slowly. It hovered
in the air between us.

"Keep it up," he said and then turned and walked out.

When the door closed shut behind him, a decorative
plate that hung high on the wall fell to the floor and broke
into pieces. I tried picking up the broken shards but tears
clouded my view and I ended up cutting my finger. What
was I so upset about? Jonas was a guy. Guys sometimes get
weird even after conventional sex, so it wasn't a huge stretch
to imagine Jonas might feel weird after his solo performance. Could be he preferred the role of spectator. Maybe
jerking off in front of me made him feel too exposed.
Maybe his quick departure had nothing to do with me. Or

maybe he didn't understand that women like at least some token gesture of affection after they've had a speaking role in a guy's own live-action porno.

I wrapped the sleeve of my shirt around my bleeding finger but let the tears slide down my face. I couldn't remember the last time I had cried and couldn't believe these tears were triggered by not getting a good night kiss from a man I had no interest in seeing again.

And that's when Victor's word "increments" popped into my brain and hit me with a full frontal impact. This incident was just another increment in a whole series of disappointments that had been occurring for months. Only this was the one that tipped the scales hard. The bad stuff now officially outweighed the good. That was the only explanation for my weepy condition. It was either that or my boss's depression really was contagious. I decided to opt for the latter. I had to. I couldn't afford to live the examined life.

fifteen

While standing in his walk-in closet trying to decide what to wear to dinner, Mr. Famous's mood shifted. The sight of a red cashmere sweater—a Christmas gift from Daniel Cross, whom Mr F had known for twenty years—made him grumpy. Daniel's Next Wave Films had financed *Last Standing* and the sweater said everything about how unenthusiastic he was with the picture.

Holiday presents in Hollywood are always an accurate way of assessing where you are in the industry hierarchy. Especially the ones that came from Daniel. If you got one of his generic presents, it meant you had slipped in his rating system. Expensive cashmere sweaters or Italian-made leather picture frames were generous presents but they required little thought. It was like getting a basket of wine and cheese. So you got the five-hundred-dollar gift basket and a screenwriter got the seventy-five-dollar gift basket, but, basically, you were all basket cases.

On the other hand, with his A-list, Daniel got personal. He took the time to figure out something special and fabulous. He didn't go as far as Tom Cruise, who, knowing of his *Days of Thunder* costar Robert Duvall's love of horses, gifted him with a racer. But, unquestionably, everyone on Daniel's A-list was always glad to see one of his presents under their tree.

Mr. F picked up the red cashmere sweater and held onto it for a moment. Top-of-the-line fine cashmere. It was a soft, nice thing but it came with a rough message. Your star power has lost wattage, it screamed. Dim bulb. Dim bulb. Dim bulb.

From anyone else, he might be able to chalk it up to bad judgment, but Daniel was known for his brilliant mind. He may not have a lot of patience for the creative process, but he understood how things worked in Hollywood and had an uncanny ability to assess whether a career was waxing or waning long before anyone else caught on.

Fuck him, Mr. F thought as he tossed the sweater up on a shelf and then shoved it behind a stack of other fine cashmeres until there wasn't a sliver of red in sight.

Dressed in black pants and a Prada shirt, Mr. F went into the kitchen to get a drink. He loved seeing his big deep-freeze stainless steel refrigerator with double glass doors and everything inside neatly arranged. Of all the fancy things he had in his house, including a pricey Henry Moore sculpture out in the garden, it was this appliance that he appreciated the most. He opened it up and stared at the neatly arranged array of foods. It was Lucinda's doing.

She brought order into his chaotic world and it calmed him down. So much so that he forgot he came downstairs thinking he needed a drink. And by the time the phone rang, a minute later, he'd even forgotten about the red cashmere sweater.

It was Stephanie, a girl he saw from time to time, but who didn't interfere with his relationship with Claire.

"Hey there, handsome," she said, "when am I going to see your beautiful face?"

Though he smiled, not immune to the compliment, it also made him wonder how many other guys she'd said the exact same thing to. It sounded like a line that had proven to work so well it was now used indiscriminately.

"I've got my daughter this weekend," he said.

Stephanie was smart enough not to be fooled by that fact, because if a guy wants to see you, he finds a way. His daughter wasn't a child. She was a teenager, with friends of her own. She had phone calls to make, videos to watch. He didn't have to baby-sit her. But Stephanie decided not to point any of that out. "It's supposed to rain on Monday. You know how bad weather brings out the naughty girl in me. Maybe I can stop by."

He laughed. Her proposition wasn't especially funny but Stephanie had a way about her that made it easy to laugh. Somehow she managed to operate with such a light touch you didn't have to worry about not going along with her request. When talking to her, Mr. F often felt as if he were reading lines from a romantic comedy. She was also the most low-maintenance woman he'd ever dealt with, which made life easy for him, but for reasons he didn't quite understand, made him respect her less. Still, he didn't want to lose his access in case he was in the mood some other rainy Monday.

"I've got meetings," he lied. "But I really want to see you soon." And then to change the subject, he said, "What have you been up to?"

"Shopping," she replied. "I found a great vintage coat—Ossie Clark. It was outrageous but I had to go for it."

Mr. F didn't get the vintage thing. He didn't care if it was vintage Ossie Clark, vintage Chanel or vintage anybody else. Vintage meant old. Who'd want to wear a stranger's clothes, much less old clothes?

"Maybe I can wear it over to see you soon." She laughed and added, "With nothing on underneath."

He didn't want to mention that other women had already made that entrance. Many of them, over the years. He didn't want to hurt her feelings, or discourage her appetites, so he said, "We'll plan on it."

He was glad to get off the call quickly and without any drama. As he placed the phone on the counter he noticed a bowl of Pink Lady apples—his favorite. He helped himself to one and took a big bite. It tasted just the way he liked them. Not yet fully ripe and very sweet.

sixteen

spent most of the flight back to L.A. reading a Ross
Macdonald mystery. *The Zebra-Striped Hearse.* I no
longer identified with his street-smart detective, Lew
Archer, but felt more and more like one of the aimless,
formless characters Lew had to deal with. "A woman who
had seen too many changes and hadn't been changed by any
of them" is how Macdonald described one of the dames
who littered the southern California landscape. Although
formlessness is perfectly acceptable in L.A., it does come
with a price. At that moment the price was a constant low-
level anxiety, the kind you might experience if passing
through mild but relentless turbulence.

Victor had barely spoken to me since leaving the inn
and he'd taken a sleeping pill before the plane taxied out of
the gate. He didn't say a word about Layla, though I knew
they'd spent the night together. I heard her exit his room
around eight A.M. I didn't mention the Jonas incident because it wasn't my finest hour and I had no idea how my
boss would react. He might get paternalistic and say some-

thing to make me feel better. Or he might take the position that bringing Layla's boyfriend to my room, which was just two doors away from where he and Layla were fucking, was at best stupid and at worst disloyal.

Maybe the sleeping pill was a good idea. Victor and I were probably both too fragile to discuss anything other than what I was making for dinner that night. That is, if I still had a job. Nothing would have surprised me at that point. Getting terminated or getting promoted—though I didn't know to what—seemed like equal possibilities. Victor's crack-up had made him more trigger-happy than usual. He'd fire off orders or make snap decisions based on anything from his daily horoscope to something he saw on a billboard. His mood swings had gotten worse over the course of our little trip and there was no telling which mood I'd be dealing with when he finally woke up.

A car was waiting at LAX to take us to Victor's house. It was mid-afternoon, sunny but not all that warm. Commonplace for early March. Victor and I, again, sat on opposite sides of the backseats, looking out our respective windows. He was a bit more talkative now but something strange had happened. When he'd awoken about ten minutes before landing, there seemed to have been a shift, not so much in mood as in personality. He went to sleep a self-obsessed movie star and woke up interested in everything but himself. He marveled at a passenger wearing a red fisherman's hat. He was mesmerized by the chaos of baggage claim. Was this the second stage of the crack-up? Some kind of dissociation that rendered him an observer enthralled by everyday phenomena, like a patient who'd only recently recovered his sight? What would Dr. Davenport say? I made a mental note to ask him the next time I could afford a session.

As we drove up La Cienega Boulevard, slowing down near the entrance to the 405 freeway, Victor nudged me.

"Look at that," he said as we passed a moving van in the process of loading up furniture from a low-rent apartment building. A tricycle and a shabby couch were left on the sidewalk as the movers struggled with a mattress with stains on it. "What if they're moving to a worse place? Ever think about that when you see a moving van in a place like this? Ever think about how most people live?"

"What do you mean?" I replied. "I *am* most people. Ever see how I live?" It wasn't a run-down apartment house next to the freeway, but prior to fleeing my stalker ex-boyfriend, home was a tiny house on a canyon road that turned into a river whenever it rained. The place also had bad plumbing and needed a paint job.

Victor wasn't buying it. "You've got to start looking at why you judge yourself by what you don't have rather than what you could have."

There was something in what he said that rang true. "Is that what I've got to start looking at?" I was flattered that he even thought about my life enough to have an opinion. However, it was a conversation I could only have, and would only have, with Dr. Davenport, so I handled the moment by playfully mocking him.

"Are you judging my judgments?"

He thought about it for a moment before answering. "Yeah, probably. Though who am I to . . ." He paused again before adding, "Tell you what. I owe you one. You get a shot at judging me. Say whatever you think. Get it off your chest. Go ahead, finish this sentence. 'You've got to start looking at . . .' "

I laughed. "No, no, no. That's a dangerous game for an employee to play with her boss."

To move off the tricky topic, I took out my cell phone to check my messages. There was a call from Rita, the chef who worked for Saint Daniel, asking for my recipe for shrimp risotto. Claire called inviting me to have lunch with her. *What?* Why would she want to have lunch with me? We weren't friends and I wasn't going to spy on Victor. I felt like a traitor even getting her message and quickly hit 3 to delete it from my voice mail. The remaining four calls were all hang-ups. My guess was they were from my stalker.

I handed my cell to Victor. "Do you want to check your messages?"

"Not really," he said, but did anyway, fast-forwarding through a number of them until one got his attention. It was a bad-news call, judging by the frown, which settled on his brow as if it would never leave.

"What's wrong?"

"A call from Alex. Now the reshoots have been canceled."

"That's good, right? You didn't want to do them anyway."

"It's bad. It probably means they're going to dump the movie. Minimum ad campaign. No TV support. Probably not even a fucking billboard."

The last time he'd had to deal with discouraging news about his movie, he'd tossed his cell phone out the window. Worried that he would now toss mine, I anxiously eyed his grip on my Nokia.

He surprised me with further evidence that he'd awakened with a personality change. He calmly snapped the phone shut and handed it back to me.

"Nothing's worse than failing low, Luce."

If true, why was he smiling? Who was this calm stranger? Did leaving behind memories of a dead brother and heading home to an almost dead movie career explain this new attitude?

The car took a right off the crowded commercial stretch of Pico Boulevard, and headed north to the more spacious neighborhoods up in the hills.

"Sometimes when they take everything away from you, it's a good thing. Clears away the junk. Lets you see where you are. What you have to do next."

The emphasis on the last sentence left no doubt that Victor had some kind of scheme in the works. Oh God, I thought, is he thinking constructively or going deeper into craziness?

To avoid dwelling on my paranoid vision of his scary plan, I said, "You're going to have look at why you'd fast-forward through all the friendly messages to get to the bad one."

He laughed. "I like this game."

"What game?"

He didn't answer because at that moment he spotted another moving van stopped on the side of the road.

seventeen

As Mr. F pulled up to Claire's house, the clock on the dashboard of his Hummer read 8:05 P.M. She flew out the front door before he could turn off the engine.

"You're late," she said as she got inside. "As always." His habitual tardiness always annoyed her, but annoyed her beyond restraint when he showed up driving that thing. Why couldn't he show up in his Porsche instead of a piece of equipment designed for the Gulf War? It's not as if they were going off-road. They were barely going off Sunset. Just a few blocks south to The Ivy on Robertson, for God's sake. Her displeasure was palpable.

"Something wrong?" Mr. F asked.

She took a moment before answering, as if the effort needed to respond was more of an investment in the conversation than she cared to make.

"Have you ever looked in your rearview mirror and seen

one of these metal monsters behind you? They look positively evil."

"Metal monster?" He held back a grin and changed the
subject. "You look beautiful," he said, because she did and
also because he knew that the fifteen-minute ride to the
restaurant would be fifteen minutes too long if Claire
started channeling her socialite Connecticut mother. Her
snotty boarding school accent would become more pro-
nounced as she postulated on evil Hummers and why keeping people waiting was a sign of inferior breeding.

And if he argued with her, explaining that they were
riding in one of the finest pieces of automotive ingenuity
and that showing up fifteen minutes late was not considered
tardy in this town, she'd change tactics and say, "Let's drop
it and try to have a good time." That switcheroo from bitch
to martyr would set him off. Get him going on all the manipulative women out there. If pushed too hard he might
fire back, telling Claire that fancy accents and breeding
didn't matter. It all came down to the same thing. Manipulative women didn't make his dick hard.

By the time they pulled up to the valets, Claire was
calmer. The thought of the Ivy gimlet she'd be drinking in
a few minutes helped a lot, as did the attention she got for
arriving with a movie star. Unfortunately, this wasn't
enough to completely wipe out the nagging feeling that
men like Victor had too many options for her own good.

eighteen

We'd been back in L.A. for a week before the next crisis hit. I should have known. It had been too quiet. Not a peep from my ex-boyfriend stalker. I was beginning to feel safe enough to return to my own house. Victor had been low-key to the point where life in the mansion was beginning to get a little boring. He was now spending a lot of time in his "at home" office, sitting in front of the computer creating a website. Yeah, that's what the world needs, another vanity website. The shock was that *he* was doing it. Pre–crack-up he'd have had the best techie out of the Silicon Valley creating it for him. Victor and a how-to manual was a whole new experience. He didn't talk about what he was doing or talk about much of anything else. Although we did keep his latest favorite pastime going. Every once in a while he or I would say, *You really should look into, etc.* It was a way of communicating serious thoughts without being serious. As games go this one was pretty useful for two fragile people who even in healthy times had trouble speaking and hearing the truth.

It was my fault that the peace was broken. I unintentionally brought the crisis into the house inside a grocery bag from the Beverly Glen Market. I'd picked up a copy of *The Star* because there was an item in the gossip pages about Shane, the director of Victor's troubled movie. The item showed the director out with a young sexy film star. I'd heard Victor talk about the guy and knew he liked him. He felt a kinship to the young filmmaker because he was smart, cool and hated the same studio executives that Victor did. I thought it'd be good for my boss to see that his director was out enjoying himself in spite of the studio's plan to dump the movie.

In my haste to get the fat-free frozen yogurt into the freezer, I handed the paper to Victor without checking to see if there were any potentially upsetting items among that week's stories. It could be anything, a rumor about his love life or some sordid speculation about an incident in his past. When you work for a movie star, especially one whose mental state is delicately balanced, the weekly tabloids are not something you cavalierly bring into the home. If I hadn't gotten caught up with making room in the fridge so I could neatly stack the three different types of lettuce I'd bought for that night's dinner salad, I might have been alert enough to run interference.

I guess the peace and quiet of the week had knocked away my defenses. There I was, disarmed and humming away as Victor flipped through the pages. Unpacking the second grocery bag, I pulled out a jug of detergent that Anna, the housekeeper, had asked me to pick up and I carried it into the laundry room.

I was in there for maybe thirty seconds, as long as it took

for me to make room for the super-sized Cheer on the supply shelf. By the time I got back to the kitchen, Victor was gone. *The Star* was on the table, opened to a page I hadn't read. A small photo of Claire and Victor caught my attention. She was smiling and wearing a fancy dress, probably a snap from some party or premiere. Beneath the shot was one paragraph that read:

After Claire Neville's drive off a Mulholland cliff earlier this year, you might think she'd make a good candidate for the next episode of "Survivor." But the jewelry designer/photographer and ex-girlfriend of Victor Mason has a new calling: Producer. She's just optioned *Skate*, a novel she plans on turning into her first feature, which she's already set up with Daniel Cross at Next Wave Films. And no, she won't be asking her famous ex to play the lead.

As I got to the last sentence, I heard Victor's Porsche backing out of the garage. By the time he passed the kitchen window he was already in second gear and grinding into a hard third.

nineteen

made the salad anyway, just in case he'd be back in time for dinner. I had to do something other than just sit there and count off the minutes to what was becoming the longest afternoon of my life, as well as the most schizophrenic. I went back and forth. First I'd tell myself not to overreact, that Victor was fine. Of course he was furious. That book *Skate* was his passion. If I knew that, certainly Claire knew that and also knew that ambushing him on the project was a surefire way to get his attention. But Victor had returned from Cape Cod more detached and less combative than he'd ever been before. It was possible he would work through his anger and frustration by breaking a few speed limits and that's all. At any moment, I told myself, he'll be back, no harm done, except for maybe an expensive traffic ticket. Or maybe not even that. It's not like cops in L.A. were immune to the charms of action stars.

As soon as I started to relax for a second, my thoughts would swing to a darker scenario. It was also possible Victor had gone to Claire's house and they were at that very moment embroiled in a huge fight. Very possible, considering the last time they were together Claire ended up flying off a canyon cliff, with a gun that'd recently been fired hidden inside the glove compartment. As time passed, this dark scenario grew stronger.

Finally I had to do something. I threw the salad in a Tupperware bowl with an air-tight cover and put it in the refrigerator. It was still light out but it wouldn't be for long. All I wanted to hear was the sound of my boss's car coming down the driveway, but when I stepped out the door, the canyon was as quiet as if it were three A.M. As I got in my car I realized I should have left a note in case Victor returned before I did. Not wanting to slow down, I decided to leave a message with Gus, the guard at the gate. Now all I had to do was figure out exactly where I was going.

A reasonable question might be, Why did I feel I had to do something to save my boss? I wasn't his bodyguard, his girlfriend, an ex-wife, his best friend, his agent or his keeper. Another good question might be, What qualified me to be anyone's savior? The best answer I could come up with is that my sense of well-being had somehow, without me noticing when it happened, gotten twisted up with his happiness, so in effect I was saving myself. And I'm not just talking about preserving a weekly paycheck. Plus, people react all kinds of crazy, delusional ways when there's a "tear in the curtain." It's a phrase I picked up from *Fly Hard*, one of Victor's early movies. In it he plays a maverick cop who saves a socialite who's being pursued by the mob after witnessing their murder of a corrupt congressman. At the end of the film, as he's leading the woman away from the horror and back to the safety of her Upper East Side world, he reassures her that it's all going to be okay. "No," she replies. "Once there's been a tear in the curtain, it'll never be the same again. It might be awful and it might be great but it can never be the same again."

I loved that line because I've experienced lots of little tears in that curtain that separates everyday life from the madness on the other side. When they happen, they temporarily wipe out the pastel colors from your life. You feel as if all you have left is black or white, devastation or transformation.

By the way, that line was supposed to be the last scene in the movie but the studio hated it so they added a half page of banal dialogue over a sexy shot of Victor and the socialite walking away from the deadly finale arm in arm. It looked like something right out of a Tawny Kitaen/ Whitesnake video.

So there I was parked outside Claire's house, thinking about curtain tears, movies from the eighties, the fact that Victor's crack-up had affected me more than I'd first thought and the suspicious car that was parked a little ways up on the other side of the street. It was a Chevy Nova, which stood out in this neighborhood of SUVs and BMWs. I couldn't make out much about the driver, except that she was female and had been there when I arrived and was still there twenty minutes later.

Yes, for twenty minutes I waited. For what? Claire wasn't home (I'd rung the doorbell) and Victor's car wasn't around.

There seemed no good reason to park myself outside Claire's million-dollar bungalow except that when there's been a tear in the curtain, it's hard to tell a good reason from a bad. My thinking was that if Victor showed up in a volatile mood I could talk him into leaving before Claire showed up and proved just how explosive a pampered princess can be when she doesn't get her way. No one needed more headlines.

The longer I sat there, the more disturbed I became by that suspicious car. Even if it was just some weirdo, it could be a weirdo who might witness an action star losing control of his testosterone. Or worse, a weirdo with a camera who could sell the snapshot. I could picture Victor's enraged face staring out at me from *The Enquirer*. You can't be too careful about this kind of thing when you live in L.A. I knew I had to investigate even though I wasn't happy with the new role I'd been thrust into. Just call me the accidental detective.

Though not yet dark, the sun was long gone and the twilight gave even the neatly cropped hedges a sinister look. As I walked toward the suspicious car, a dog started barking from behind a tall wooden fence. The lights inside the suspicious car were turned on and then quickly turned off. In that moment of illumination I got a glimpse of the driver. Big blond hair. That's all I could tell for sure. A female with big blond hair. Not much to work with for a composite sketch.

As I neared the parked car, I looked down at the ground to find something to protect myself with . . . a rock or a broken branch, but I found nothing. Damn these neighborhoods that get their streets cleaned twice a week. When I looked up again, just as I was about even with the Chevy, I glanced over to the driver's side expecting to see this big-haired woman staring back at me. What I saw was nothing. No one. Where did she go? There had been no sound of a car door opening or footsteps, which only made it even more freakish. A braver detective would have gone over to the window and peered inside but that was a little too advanced for me. I needed backup or I needed to back off. Where was the fucking neighborhood security patrol? This was a job for guys with guns and police radios.

I did a one-eighty and headed back to my car. The dog was still barking, and now from across the canyon, a second started up. Not my favorite duet. As I got closer to my Jeep, I became aware of someone behind me. I didn't know if I should turn and look or keep going. I pulled the keys out of my pocket and unlocked the driver's-side door as I felt a hand grab my arm.

I tore myself away and jumped back only to be greeted by a peal of laughter. It was Claire.

"That was quite a reaction."

She did not ask what I was doing there, which would be my first question if I came home to find my ex-boyfriend's chef lurking in the shadows. Claire seemed remarkably composed.

"Have you been home all this time?" I asked.

"All what time?"

"I rang the bell," I replied, not wanting to admit I'd been hanging around there for a half hour.

"I went on a hike."

"It's dark out."

"I stopped at my neighbor's." As she talked she led the

way up the path to her front door. Before opening it she turned around to face me, panic in her eyes. "Is Victor okay? Did something happen to him?"

Her concern appeared genuine in spite of the fact that she'd just screwed him out of his dream project. Guess that was her version of separate issues.

"He's okay," I said, unconvincingly. As I followed Claire inside the house, my mind was racing, trying to come up with some big fat lie to explain my presence in her living room. Lew Archer had it easy. He was a licensed P.I. I was just a concerned party with poor judgment. Any second now Claire would want an explanation. I scrambled to balance my loyalty to Victor versus my concern for his welfare. I needed time to figure this one out and this time I got it. Before I could close the door behind me, a third person showed up. The female with big blond hair was joining our party.

think at this point I have to explain how the art of the lie is cultivated in Hollywood, because lying is becoming a leitmotif in this ongoing saga. There are essentially four categories of liars. At the top of the heap are the master liars who, at their core, are great performers. Beneath them are those people who have to lie for a living: agents, lawyers and publicists. Below them are those who lie compulsively though not necessarily all that well. Often this group includes drug addicts and people cheating on their spouses. And the largest but less skillful category is the one I fell into—people who lie because the truth is either an invasion of privacy or they don't have the guts for a confrontation.

Working on the fly, the best I could come up with was

that I'd found a couple of Claire's things (T-shirt, bracelet) at Victor's and I was stopping by to return them. I had seen those items somewhere in the house but couldn't even remember where. Which led me to the backup lie. "I drove over thinking I had your stuff in the backseat," I said, "but turns out I must have left it in the garage. I'd put it in a Barney's shopping bag and I remember I put the bag down to take my gym stuff out of the car. I was going to do my laundry later. I guess that Barney's bag is still sitting there."

I'm not sure she bought my story. I may have gone a little overboard with the specifics, and Claire was too savvy not to know that too many details of an explanation that's iffy to begin with usually means the storyteller is bullshitting.

"Don't worry about it," Claire said. "I can get it the next time I'm over there. When hell freezes over." She laughed and then took me by the arm and ushered me over to the living room, where the woman with big hair was assembling her tools. Turns out the driver of the suspicious car was there to give Claire her weekly "mani/pedi."

"You're a manicurist? I thought you were . . . well, I don't know what I thought."

"That I was some weirdo?"

"Kind of."

"Because that's what I thought you were. When you started walking toward me, I was going to call the cops, but then I dropped my cell phone and by the time I found it, you were walking back down the hill."

"I'm not even going to go into how crazy and paranoid I got when I passed your car and you were suddenly gone."

"Twilight up in the canyons will do that to you. It can get spooky up here."

"It is not spooky," Claire announced. "It's quiet and very well protected." She plopped down in an easy chair and took off her shoes. "Sit down, stay awhile," she said to me. "Help me pick out a color." She passed me a small basket filled with nail polishes.

I've always been amazed at Claire's high WASP style. No matter how many tears in her curtain, she always continues on with the kind of stiff upper lip made famous by the British. Claire's New England style wasn't quite that stiff, but she did have an ability to move on to the next event without a lot of public angst over what was left behind. It was all onward and upward. For a girl who had been riled up enough to drive off a cliff, she appeared to have survived without a scar. At most the incident seemed to have sparked some kind of playful battle for revenge.

"Can't, I've got to get going," I said as I picked out Chanel's "Sirene" for her toes.

"You don't have to go this minute," she replied authoritatively. Her sense of entitlement was showing and it was as tacky as fake tits in a low-cut Versace gown, which, by the way, Claire would never consider putting on her blue-blood body. "I have a question for you," she said.

"What?" I feared where this might be going, especially when Claire waited till the manicurist went to the kitchen before continuing.

"Is Victor seeing anyone special or is it just his usual parade of bimbos who will come over and blow him whenever he wants." She actually managed to say this without any obvious bile or bitterness. Her tone was as light as if asking if I preferred my nails filed square-ish or round.

"How do I know who he's seeing?"

"Because you work for him and I hear you're also living up at the house."

"I make it my business not to get into his business."

She rejected my choice of Chanel and went for the bright red Nars.

"He's lucky to have someone as loyal as you. Which is why I'm not upset that you never returned my call, though it was incredibly rude." She practically gave me a just kidding wink as she spoke, which made me even more anxious to get out of there. Her double talk was making me queasy.

"He's a pretty loyal friend, too."

She moved forward and studied my face, getting a little too close for my comfort. "You should get Randall to Botox your frown line," she said delicately, touching the spot between my eyes.

She was referring to Dr. Haworth, her plastic surgeon. Claire and all her girlfriends always referred to their plastic surgeons by their first names. It was never doctor so-and-so. It made it all seem very clubby, and judging by the indentations between my brows, not a club I could afford.

"Not in my budget," I admitted.

"Victor should pay for it. He puts lines on every woman around him."

"I arrived at the job with them," I said.

"Get 'your loyal friend' to pay anyway," she insisted as her phone rang. She was happy to reach for it because my answers were not providing much in the way of information or entertainment.

"Hey, Daniel," she said with a girlish giggle. "Hold on a minute, will you, sweetie?"

She gave me one of her smiles, the kind she probably considered gracious but which struck me as condescending. "Got to take this in the other room. If you're gone by the time I'm back, have a good one."

It was a polite dismissal but a dismissal. Now that I'd witnessed her call from Daniel she was probably hoping I'd mention it to Victor. She was probably thinking that if I wasn't going to give her any info, the least I could do was pass some along.

Before I got to the front door, the manicurist stopped me.

"He was here," she said softly. "Ten minutes before you drove up."

I didn't have to ask who—she and I spoke the same language. We were both in the service business, and years spent working with people with big bank accounts and big egos had taught us how to quickly sum up a situation with a minimum of evidence.

"How did he seem?"

"Take a look at the tire tracks he left on the lawn. He wasn't happy."

"Don't tell Claire," I said. Though I didn't even know this woman's name and had only met her minutes before, I intuitively knew that she was trustworthy.

"I'm not telling her anything. She was forty-five minutes late and didn't bother to say she was sorry."

"She'll give you a big tip to make up for it."

"A big tip buys a lot, but it doesn't buy everything."

twenty

I drove back to the house thinking about how much I disliked Claire, and it had nothing to do with jealousy. She'd probably be shocked to hear that, by my calculations, she should be jealous of me. If you think of life as a football field in terms of wealth and opportunities, I was born on the twenty-yard line, eighty yards from the goal line. With talent, effort and luck, a twenty-yarder could end up far down the field in L.A. Currently, I considered myself fifty yards from victory. I figured Claire was born fifteen yards from a win, and was now only ten yards away. She may have the better lifestyle, but she'd gained only five yards to my thirty. My snobbishness and bitchiness surfaced in this yardage contest. Which explains why, in spite of Victor's mediocre action movies and his silly macho antics (his penchant for wearing race-car-driver jackets was a bit much), I had deep respect for my boss and his humble Cape Cod beginnings, and so very little patience for the very entitled Connecticut-bred Claire. Now that I've vented, I have to add that, okay, I am a little jealous of those fabulous garnet and gold Anthony Nak earrings she was wearing. They sold for a thousand bucks at Barney's. Much too expensive for those of us stuck mid-field.

Gus was still at his post at the gate. With his protruding gut and kind face he appeared more suited to a job as Santa Claus than a security guard. As I pulled up, he stepped out from the small enclosure, barely bigger than a tollbooth, which served as his office. In the background I saw that his twelve-inch-screen TV was tuned to the nightly news.

"Did Victor get back?" I asked, knowing that technically Gus wasn't supposed to give out any information about the residents of this private enclave, not even to the employees of those residents.

"No," he said as his eyes darted to a news story about tensions in the Middle East.

"Have you been here the whole time?"

"Since four o'clock."

Finally he turned his attention back to me. "Sorry about that but I'm kind of a news junkie."

"I don't watch the news," I said, which was mostly true, but I knew if I encouraged Gus at all he'd be giving me his opinions on foreign policy.

"Ever?"

"Fear, hope, fear, hope. Don't you ever feel like it's all just one big manipulation?"

Obviously he never did because he looked at me the way he might look at some demented trespasser. "How do you keep up with what's going on?"

"I read the paper."

"You get it quicker on TV," he replied as he again concentrated on the small screen. A commercial was airing featuring an attractive young woman wearing a short, sexy business suit and very high heels. So much for the crisis in the Middle East.

I left him to his entertainment, and although he'd opened the gate for me, he may not have noticed that I didn't drive through it.

Instead, I headed east toward Laurel Canyon, stopping by the side of the road where I was sure I could get good cell phone reception. I put in a call to Dr. Davenport and left a message. It was too late in the day for him to be taking appointments, and I had no idea what his phone checking habits were. He didn't have a standard service that paged him in case of an emergency, so my hope was that he'd check in after hours. Once the call was placed I just sat there, pretty sure that if Victor returned he'd pass by the very spot where I was parked. I figured I might as well wait there for him, where I could at least look out over the rim of the canyons to a spectacular view of the Los Angeles basin. This is why so many people want to live up here, I thought. The vast panorama makes thinking big seem reasonable. That's what makes L.A. so tricky. The topography encourages you to take risks in the hope of making it big, even though a more ordered, controlled life with smaller expectations might be better for your overall health. Harsher, colder weather and no horizon might have led me to making safer choices, instead of becoming a person who doesn't have a savings account and might never have a pension plan.

Not that I grew up in the frigid Northwest. Quite the opposite. I was born in Riverside in San Bernardino County, an hour east of L.A., in a place best known for having some of the hottest temperatures in any local area that's not a desert. That day in August when I left for good was a record-breaking 113 degrees. In spite of the unbearable summer heat, people talk about Riverside as a city of the future. Every so often there'll be a flurry of interest in bringing a big sports team to the area but it never pans out. That's Riverside, the home of things not panning out. Or maybe that's just my experience, growing up with a father who made a mediocre living selling tires and a mother who spent years getting her real estate license but never sold a house. I left at eighteen in a used Toyota Camry with seventy thousand miles on the odometer but, courtesy of my dad, a brand-new set of radials.

Like everyone else who comes to Hollywood, I had ambitions and dreams but I was never a fame chaser. I simply came here hoping to live my life on my own terms, doing work I love, making a decent living doing it and never having to fuck anyone I didn't ache to fuck. This wish list might seem childish and indulgent in another climate, but there's something about L.A., especially from the perspective of a mountaintop, that makes it seem possible. Damn that beautiful panorama.

For the next half hour I sat in my car waiting for either the sight of my boss's car speeding by or a call from my shrink. It was conceivable that Dr. Davenport never checked his messages once he'd finished his day's work. If that was the case, I couldn't blame him. A full day of dealing with craziness might make him crazy, too, if he didn't disconnect from all the people who wanted some kind of fix. I tried to imagine what it must be like to have to listen to complaints and concerns all day long. I wasn't a therapist and I certainly heard my share. Lately in L.A. the big concern was mold. Suddenly everyone was worried that their house or apartment building had some toxic fungus lurking in the walls. There were also lots of worries about autoimmune disease, which as far as I could tell was a diagnosis that fit about a thousand symptoms. And given the time of year it was, there was also lots of discussion about whether or not the Oscar race had become all about Hollywood politics. I'm sure Davenport handled all of this with his usual direct approach. You didn't always get what you wanted from him but you always ended up getting what you needed. No coddling. But lots of information.

There were a number of times during that half hour when I could have easily become a serial caller, hitting that redial button with every exhale. Like many L.A. girls, I have a cell phone addiction. Often I'll be overcome with a burning need to call someone, anyone. The affliction gets really bad anytime I find myself waiting, especially at a restaurant. If a friend is five minutes late for a lunch date, chances are I've got my Nokia up to my ear by the time they walk in. I guess it's to be expected when you live in a culture in which even immediate gratification feels like Mercury in retrograde.

Once I'd passed the half-hour mark, I gave in to the urge and felt some measure of relief hearing the phone ringing on the other end. If Davenport's damned answering machine picked up again, my plan was to go back to the house and have a glass of wine and try to think about anything but this.

Surprise, surprise. Plan B was out and Plan A was on the front burner. The doctor was back in.

"It's Lucinda. Did you get my message?"

"I did," he said. I couldn't tell if that meant he did and was going to call me back or he did and purposely didn't call me back. It was possible he felt a callback would be enabling my neurotic needs.

"I was wondering if I could come by, not for a full session but maybe just a half hour of your time, though of course," I added quickly, "I'll pay the full amount."

"What's going on?" He didn't sound enthusiastic. Why should he be? I sounded like just another L.A. nutcase in a crisis over a split end.

"It's a situation with Victor." I didn't want to get into the details in case somehow, someone was able to tap into the call. It was justifiable paranoia as there had been incidents of celebrities having their private conversations picked up by scanners or overly aggressive private investigators. Ever since the Feds nabbed Anthony Pellicano, the detective to the stars, even the most innocuous click on a phone line had people talking in code.

"When did you want to come by?"

"I can be there in ten minutes."

"Make it fifteen," he said, and hung up.

I have to say I was kind of shocked he agreed. Would he have been as accommodating if the request for a session didn't involve a movie star? I cringed at the thought of it. Davenport was too smart and detached to be swayed by star power. On the other hand, he was human, and who doesn't

have at least mild curiosity when it comes to stories about
how the mighty have fallen?

The doctor worked out of his house, in his office, which
was a two-room suite over his garage. During business
hours the door was left unlocked and patients waited in the
outer area until called into the inner sanctum. I'd never
been there for an evening session before, but the routine was
the same, except when I arrived the door between the two
rooms was open and Davenport wasn't around.

I checked my watch. It was only a little after seven.
Victor usually liked to eat around eight-thirty. It was possible that I could be back in the kitchen at ten to eight.
The salad would only take another five minutes and the
fish had been marinating all day. I went through a mental checklist of what had to be done and in what order I
would do it. I made plans for an "everything is okay" scenario and an "everything is not okay" scenario. This was
my way of multitasking. And while I calculated the time
it would take to heat up the grill and mused over what
the LAPD's policy was on missing persons, Davenport
showed up.

Instead of the harsh glare that poured down from the
skylight during the day, the place felt cozy due to two table
lamps with pale amber shades. Any thoughts I might have
had about relaxing were quickly dispelled, however, by Davenport's reaction to my dilemma.

"So you're doing it again." It wasn't said in an accusa-
tory way. He was stating a fact that pertained to one of my
ongoing issues. It was fantasy bond 101. If I kept putting

my sense of well-being in the hands of a man, then I'd have no choice but to make sure that he could be counted on, even if it meant propping him up myself. I blame it on a paternalistic society, which hooks us on the need for Big Daddy in one form or another. It was territory Davenport and I had gone over several times before but that didn't stop me from challenging him.

"Maybe," I said, "I'm just concerned about someone who happens to be going through a rough time. Is that so impossible to imagine?"

Davenport cracked the slightest smile, which he often did as a way of telling me that I should know better but he'll humor me by repeating the obvious.

"That someone is the person you work for, the person who's providing you with a place to live and the person whose persona as an action hero is what drew you to him in the first place."

I could have argued his conclusion. I could have said that action flicks seem silly to me. I could have smugly added that Hong Kong–style kickboxing is visually interesting, at times beautiful, but I prefer guys who are tough without fancy editing and visual tricks.

It wasn't a very strong argument because whatever else you could say about my boss, he was very, very good at his job. Whether or not the movie was a hit, Victor always maintained an image of incredible vitality by his adventures on that celluloid landscape. The strong impression he created on the big screen lingered even when he was having a bad day and dragged himself around the house like an old man with a bad back. And I wasn't immune to feeling a little charged up by preparing a nice mushroom and spinach risotto (light on the butter) for my very own Indiana Jones.

Sometimes I wished Davenport was a bad therapist. There were times when I could have used a less ethical insightful shrink. Someone I could go to and say my boss did this, my boyfriend did that, my girlfriends are doing whatever, and he would help me formulate a winning strategy. Fuck sanity and health. At times I wanted Davenport to be part fortune-teller, part general, and on one occasion I even told him that. He laughed and said, "That would be easy compared to trying to sell people the bottom line. I'm never surprised when a patient doesn't come back for a second session."

I was brave enough to keep coming back, but I could only handle small amounts of truth at one sitting. I was like those people who daintily taste food rather than devour it. I took a small bite out of Davenport's theory about how we keep inviting the same experiences (in different disguises) into our lives over and over again until we resolve the issue at the core of our attachment. In other words, why was I always around men who disappeared on me—in one way or another—and why was Victor always involved with crazy women?

The closer Davenport got to this issue, the more I started thinking about all the reasons I needed to cut the session short. I was thinking the fish would taste better if I fired up the outdoor grill. Davenport was talking mental health and I was thinking mesquite. Usually it's the therapist who checks his watch to signal the session is up, but I was the one glancing at my wrist. There was time for one more question so I asked what he could conclude from Victor's sudden interest in all that was commonplace, especially moving vans.

Davenport leaned back in his chair, a sign that he was about to launch into one of his stories. "I had a patient in here yesterday who is recovering from major surgery. Hollywood girl. Thirty years old. The last fifteen have been pretty much a nonstop party, till this medical problem happened. She's fine now, but for about a month she didn't know if she would be. During those thirty days she became enamored of her next-door neighbor, who is an eye doctor. Twice a week she'd come to see me and tell me about the joys of staying home with him, ordering takeout and watching back-to-back episodes of 'Law and Order.' A week after she was given a clean bill of health, she fell in love with a nineteen-year-old drummer in a rock band."

"Okay, got it," I said. "But I'm not sure how I feel about it."

"That depends," he laughed. "Do you see yourself as the doctor or the drummer?"

"Neither," I lied. I handed him a check. "One more thing. What if he isn't back by tomorrow morning? Should I call the police?"

"Call his agent," Davenport replied quickly, as if he'd been asked this question a thousand times before.

Of course he was right. This is Hollywood. People go AWOL all the time. Stars sneak off to Palm Springs or Santa Barbara. They head south to Cabo or north to Big Sur. And if Alex, an agent known for being one of the best problem solvers in the business, couldn't find Victor, he'd at least know how to find a real-life Lew Archer to track him down.

twenty-one

f the Ivy's specials are always the same every night, why do they call them specials?" Claire directed the comment to the waiter as he brought the second round of drinks to the table.

"People ask me that all the time," the young man replied, placing Claire's gimlet in front of her with a smile. She didn't smile back. He had given the wrong answer. Claire thought she was being funny and astute, not just one of dozens who came before her who had made the exact same observation.

"And the answer would be . . . ?" She picked the piece of mint out of her drink and licked the end of it.

The waiter shrugged, but Lawrence had an answer. "Because it's a test to see if you're listening. It's a little game the waiters have going."

It was something he came up with to shut her up. He usually enjoyed Claire's liveliness but lately he noticed that she became surly whenever she was out in public with

Mr. Famous. It was as if she got frustrated by not being a star herself and was taking it out on waiters, parking valets and, tonight, his date, Rikki.

From an outsider's perspective that table for four probably seemed glamorous. Mr. Famous wasn't Brad Pitt or Tom Cruise, but he was a genuine star. Claire wasn't Julia Roberts or Angelina Jolie, but she was a beautiful woman who dressed better than actresses with full-time stylists on the payroll. Lawrence's glam quotient came with his rugged good looks, reminiscent of a young Peter Beard. And though his job as a music business attorney didn't come close to Beard's exotic life as a roving photographer, he shared Beard's taste for model/actresses. Rikki, the one joining him that night, wasn't anyone whose face ever stared out from the pages of *Vogue,* nor was her list of screen credits very long or impressive. However, she was pretty, and her day job as a private fitness trainer accounted for her spectacular body. To an uneducated eye, this foursome might look enviable, but insiders—half the diners at the Ivy that night—would see it differently.

They'd immediately pick up on the fact that Claire barely spoke to Rikki and that Rikki was dressed to express herself, and unfortunately all she had to say was I've got a great body. They'd notice that Lawrence was working hard to keep everybody happy and that Mr. Famous had knocked back two drinks before the main course arrived, which some observers would conclude was not a good sign and so "eighties" of him. If Mr. Famous had a chance to defend himself, he might have pointed out that these same critics were more than happy to participate full force in the good old eighties, back when it was good business to encourage excess.

Back when partying in public was considered cool and people would drive farther east than they'd ever been before to get to Helena's, a club that hit the town's eighties zeitgeist perfectly. When Mr. Famous cruised by there on his first night in L.A., he didn't have the cachet to get past the doorman. Two years later, when he was an up-and-comer, he regularly hung out at one of the best tables in the house, the one next to Jack's. Back then people didn't count how many drinks you had. Now they practically counted the ice cubes in your glass, as if drinking your vodka straight up made you a more likely candidate for AA.

Though Mr. Famous was well aware that whatever he did was watched and commented on, he usually took it as a compliment, not an intrution. Not that night. He would have preferred dining in the corner of the back room, oblivious to all commentary, but Claire had requested the high-profile patio. He should have said something when they arrived but Lawrence and his date looked so settled, cuddled close on the upholstered couch that served as the seating for that number-one table. Instead Mr. F kept his thoughts to himself and took a seat facing the wall, his back to all curious eyes, which is how he got blindsided by Stephanie.

There she was unabashedly tapping him on the shoulder and grinning. To her credit she didn't say, I thought you were spending time with your daughter. She did not make a big deal, or any kind of deal, about the fact that he'd lied to her and, with very little ceremony, blew her off. There wasn't a drop of anger or sarcasm in her voice.

"I don't want to interrupt your dinner, just wanted to say hi."

Survivors like Stephanie understand the rules of the

Hollywood game and always find a way to abide by them without feeling like a doormat. It's Hollywood alchemy. Take the downside of being involved with a celebrity and find a way to be energized by it. She took pride in being able to handle whatever came down that red carpet graciously. She may not like it, but the act—at times, the art of handling it—assured her some self-respect.

Claire, being a relative newcomer to the town and an East Coast princess, would never understand that dance. At that moment all she understood was that there was another woman encroaching on her territory. She may not have been well versed in the L.A. girl's guide to dating alpha males, but her intuition served her well. By the time her lobster was brought to the table Claire had completely lost her appetite. Oh, fuck it, she thought, and ordered another gimlet.

twenty-two

The Grill in Beverly Hills is the current power lunch spot for the Hollywood crowd, in part because of its perfect location. United Talent Agency is across the street. William Morris is just a couple of blocks away. CAA is within walking distance, and ICM is no more than a five-minute drive—even in traffic. The Grill's interior, which is conducive to a boys club, looks like something you might find on Boston's Beacon Hill rather than a few steps away from Euro-trendy Rodeo Drive. Booths are made of dark wood and green leather. The lighting fixtures are faux antiques. There are no windows.

Women enter this male bastion at lunchtime mostly for business or, on occasion, husband shopping. There's a famous story about a woman named Jocelyn who started scheduling girlfriend lunches at The Grill, right after her last divorce. It was no secret she was on the hunt for a replacement meal ticket, except possibly to the producer she eventually snagged. By her second lunch there, she'd targeted him as a possibility and found a mutual friend to introduce them. Though she was no longer at the height of her beauty and his power in the industry had been slipping for some time—he never got seated in the VIP booths along the wall to the right—they were both very good at faking it.

The Grill was not my scene, not only because I wasn't in the business and wasn't shopping for a husband, but also because I had once had an incident there. Months before, I'd stopped by to visit a friend who worked at a boutique nearby. On my way back to my car I had to walk past The Grill and decided to pop in there and get a Cobb salad to go. No blue cheese, I said emphatically. As the waiter jotted down my order, he nodded his head as if to say I know my job, don't worry, relax. Which I did until I got home and discovered they'd crumbled blue cheese all over the top of the salad.

Usually I can roll with things, even if it means tossing the fifteen-dollar salad down the garbage disposal and eating a peanut butter and jelly sandwich, which was all I had in the house. But I'd been looking forward to that salad all the way home, through forty minutes of traffic (there'd been an accident on Laurel Canyon), and I had had enough disappointments that day and didn't need another. Plus, I absolutely hated blue cheese, which is out of character for a chef. Most food people swoon over it, describing it as aromatic and distinctive, but I just hate everything about it. The way it tastes, looks and especially the way it smells. So I picked up the phone, called the manager of the restaurant and threw a small fit. I insisted they deliver the salad the way I ordered it. Well, there was no way they were going to do that. The manager explained they weren't equipped to make home deliveries, though I'm sure if Tom Hanks called they'd deliver it and throw in a free bottle of good wine as an apology. This is what I got—a promise that they'd mail me a check for the cost of the salad. Weeks later I got a letter (no check included) telling me that the next time I came into the restaurant they'd comp my lunch. Thanks but no thanks. Something about that letter conjured up an image of me sitting at The Grill paying for my meal with coupons. It was irrational but I couldn't fake my way out of the feeling, so I tossed the letter in the trash and crossed The Grill off my list. Until I had no choice but to return.

lex, Victor's agent, had lunch there almost every day. Phoning him would have only gotten me a spot on his callback list. I needed immediate results. Victor hadn't returned to the house the night before, so at noon the next day I was on my way down the hill. Everyone who knew Alex knew he was a creature of habit, and if you knew him well enough, you knew 12:30 was his lunchtime.

It was unseasonably hot that day and I was wearing a denim skirt and didn't notice till I was walking in that my favorite James Perse T-shirt had a coffee stain on the sleeve. Great. I love looking like a conspicuous loser at an industry hot spot. Plus, I was early, so I had no choice but to sit at the bar and order an iced tea. The place was pretty quiet and would be until it got jammed around one o'clock. The manager was on the phone when I walked in and showed no sign that he recognized me as the girl who threw a fit over a Cobb salad. He probably dismissed me as a nobody who he hoped was there to meet a somebody.

Over the next fifteen minutes a handful of people strolled in, and judging by the reception they got, they were all regulars. I felt completely out of place but at least I wasn't bored. I'm always fascinated by power players in Hollywood. Not because I envy them their jobs or their money or their big houses on L.A.'s west side, but because they seem to actually believe that they are where everyone else in the world would like to be. It's as if they took the world's obsession with celebrities and their own proximity to those stars to mean that they are members of some royal court. They aren't all wrong. Of course, scratch the surface and you get a lot of guys worried that they are just a few bad deals away from being banished. Arrogance and panic in the same package is the name of that show.

As the clock hit 12:35, Alex walked in. The Grill's manager greeted him as if he, of all the members of the court, had the king's ear. As Alex headed over to his booth— along the wall on the right—I took my shot. I grabbed his arm.

"Hey, Alex."

"Hello there," he said. He was being courteous but not about to slow down.

"Can I talk to you for a second?"

He stopped. "Go," he said.

Go? I felt like he'd turned on a timer and I had to beat the clock. "This may not be any of my business but Victor may have disappeared."

"What do you mean?"

I explained the sequence of events to him.

He let it sink in for a second or two while he used his clenched fist to lightly tap on the bar's countertop. Knowing how he liked to eat on time, I felt bad keeping him from his schedule. "He's fine," he said, scanning the room quickly.

"So you've talked to him today?"

"No. But he's fine. I'll take care of this when I get back to my office."

Alex could have been as much or more concerned than I was, but he wasn't the kind of guy who would show it.

"Enjoy your lunch, dear," he said, and walked away.

I had passed on the baton of responsibility. I should have felt some degree of relief, but in fact felt worse.

I intended to pay for my iced tea and get out of there, but when I tried to get the bartender's attention, a guy sitting at the next bar stool got mine.

"It's the pine nut girl," he said.

It was Shane, the director of Victor's troubled new movie. He'd been to the house once for a meeting and I had made lunch, which, I now remembered, included pasta (made from rice flour, not wheat), broccoli and pine nuts. We were introduced and he complimented me on the food but that didn't necessarily mean he'd remember me. There have been people I've served a three-course meal to who've chatted with me at length about everything from cooking to their current personal dramas, and the very next day when I run into them at Starbucks or someplace, they don't have a clue who I am. I've learned that bonding with Victor's guests doesn't necessarily translate to even a polite hello outside the kitchen. Which is why Shane surprised and delighted me. The delight had more to do with what a sexy, brooding (in a good way) guy he was.

"Pine nut girl? I've had better nicknames," I said.

"I'm sure you have," he laughed suggestively.

"You don't need a nickname because you're blessed with a good name to start with. Doesn't get much better than Shane."

"You don't think it sounds too much like a cowboy?"

"It works in L.A. After all, this is still the wild west."

The bartender refilled my iced tea and put a Bloody Mary in front of Shane.

"Is your lunch date late?" I asked. It was either that or he needed a hit of vodka to deal with being ignored by the industry heavyweights filling up the room.

He stirred his drink. "A no-show."

"Who would not show up for you?"

"Someone who mistakenly told me the reservation was at The Grill when in fact it's at The Palm—which is where he is now."

Shane's cell was on the bar—red light blinking but the ringer volume had been turned so low it was hard to hear in the noisy Grill.

"Your phone's ringing," I said.

"It's probably the guy at The Palm calling again. Let him sweat."

But as the light kept flashing, Shane reconsidered. Maybe he was being compassionate or maybe he was hoping it was someone else. "Hello."

The look on his face said it was The Palm guy.

"We'll do it another time," Shane said. "Don't worry about it. Yeah. Sure. Have your assistant call my assistant." He rolled his eyes, letting me know he knew how bullshit it all sounded. When he hung up, he explained. "A junior executive trying to keep me happy while they kill my movie. I think they're afraid I might talk to the media."

It was not a topic he wanted to dwell on.

"Where's your lunch date?" he asked, as he checked out a few more "players in training" as they were led to less prestigious tables on the other side of the partition that separated them from the VIPs in the booths.

"Don't have one. I just stopped by to give someone a message."

He handed me the menu he'd been perusing. "I owe you a meal."

"You don't owe me anything."

"Okay, then you owe me."

"I owe you? For what?"

"For getting me hooked on pine nuts."

It may have been a silly line but it worked. It hooked me into sticking around.

There's something about a great Bloody Mary and a guy who is keeping alive my Michael Hutchence fantasy that can make me stupid. My sanity and common sense were put on hold while I engaged in a very pubic flirtation with someone I barely knew. Shane was as good-looking as Hutchence but in a different way. He had the black Irish thing going. Dark hair, light skin, blue eyes. He was probably around thirty-one or thirty-two and had the kind of powerful sexuality and rock 'n' roll vitality that rendered all debate superfluous. I felt that saying no to him would be the equivalent of taking a vow of chastity. The only way I could turn off my attraction to him was to shut down my libido completely.

Over a lunch of filet of sole and salad, we created what

would have been a mini scandal had either one of us been famous enough to get anyone's attention. Though Shane had directed my boss's movie, it was his first feature, a job he'd earned for having directed so many slick commercials. Although many of the players at The Grill knew who he was, the buzz on his movie wasn't good, so the bad-boy behavior he engaged in with me had very little gossip value. We weren't obscene but at one point he offered me a small julienne green bean from his salad, which I ate out of his hand and thanked him by licking his finger. Those Bloody Marys were strong.

But what really clinched my attraction to Shane was what happened when Glynnis, a struggling producer, walked by. She was currently number one on my enemies list because of what she'd done to my friend Elizabeth West.

"Ugh, that woman," I said. "She and people like her are the reason Compazine is such a popular drug in this town."

Shane laughed. "That stomach churning?"

"Beyond," I said, and then filled him in on the details.

Glynnis worked with Kirk, a director who had been moderately successful doing quirky movies. The previous fall, Elizabeth had been working with the two of them on her spec script and the trio planned on getting it to Renée Zellweger. Cut to a few months ago—before the Claire Neville incident—when I prepared a dinner for my boss and a few guests. As I was clearing the dishes off the table, I picked up snippets of their conversation, including a tidbit dropped by Kirk's agent, who mentioned that his client had just finished his own spec script and was getting it out to Renée that weekend.

Translation—they'd kept Elizabeth on hold for months

and were now blowing her off without so much as a courtesy phone call. Had Glynnis been at that table I think I would have poured the remains of the broiled red snapper and broccoli rabe all over her head.

I knew for a fact that in order to get attached to Elizabeth's script, Glynnis had done a full-court press. You can imagine the hype and promises that spew out of the mouth of a desperate producer trying to keep her hand in the game. I also knew as of five o'clock that afternoon, when I spoke to Elizabeth, that she was completely unaware of any change in plans. Of course I called her as soon as I had a free moment. She was philosophical about the news, but I'm not that mature.

"It's hard not to feel at least a small wave of nausea when faced with another example of spineless duplicity," I confessed to Shane. "If Glynnis had just been straightforward and said, 'Look, we're going to shop Kirk's script to Renée instead of yours because we only have one shot with her and we'd rather take it with Kirk's script,' that would still be bad but it wouldn't be quite as sickening."

I looked over to the stairs that led up to the ladies' room. I was ready to give Glynnis the evilest of eyes when she descended. "I swear," I added, "I want to have a T-shirt made up that says GIVE TRUTH A CHANCE."

"Feisty one, aren't you?" Shane said. "But why are you pissed off at this Glynnis person? She's probably just following the director's instructions. Probably too scared of losing her job not to. Get pissed off at Kirk. He's the warden, she's just part of the general population."

Love that description. In fact I loved it so much and loved him for being able to come up with it that I ordered another drink and temporarily forgot that young directors who have a Michael Hutchence quality about them date actresses, not chefs. I could picture him with Naomi Watts or someone with her degree of success and beauty. And the second I realized that, I loosened up. No reason to fear emotional intimacy when you're attracted to a guy who is clearly beyond your reach.

I let myself get so distracted and entertained that not only didn't I notice that Glynnis had passed us by on her way back to her table, but I had missed Alex's exit as well. His booth was empty, which reminded me of what had brought me there in the first place. I made a serious effort to repress the effects of the alcohol. "I've got to get going," I said.

Shane seemed surprised by my abrupt change in mood. "What are you cooking up tonight?"

The way he asked made it seem as if he wondered if I'd be in the mood to cook up a little trouble.

"I don't know yet," I said. "I'll figure it out when I get to the grocery store."

"Are you one of those cooks who can take any three ingredients and come up with something tasty?"

"Not any three. I'm a snob when it comes to quality." Though I didn't mean that to sound flirtatious, I have a feeling it did.

Shane signaled to the waiter for the check as I searched through my bag for my wallet.

"Yeah, like that's going to happen." He pushed away the two twenties in my hand and slapped down a credit card. "But you can tell me how to find you."

"I'd rather give you the forty bucks. I'm joking," I quickly added. I borrowed a pen from the bartender and wrote down my cell number on a cocktail napkin.

He gave me a kiss goodbye. "See you, gorgeous," he said.

In my old denim skirt and T-shirt I wasn't expecting any compliments but that didn't mean I didn't need one. I had a feeling Shane called a lot of girls gorgeous though I decided not to dwell on that.

When I stepped outside, the heat was oppressive but I was feeling upbeat. My boss was missing. My life was in turmoil. And even if I'd just had a lovely flirtation with a young director who was keeping the Michael Hutchence legacy alive, I knew it wasn't a flirtation that would go anywhere. Still, I felt optimistic, and that's when I thought about the book *Skate*. All I knew about the story was what Victor had told me, which had something to do with *still* having joy in your life, in spite of whatever. *Still. In spite of.* "The two linchpins that keep the wheel on the road," he'd explained. He was quoting his brother.

I had a sudden desire to read the book because as good as I felt at that moment, it occurred to me that the only two linchpins that ever kept my wheel on the road were sex and shopping and it was possible they wouldn't hold up too well on a bumpy drive.

twenty-three

Why was it her job to talk to the bimbo? That's what Claire was fuming about while Victor and Lawrence talked about college basketball. She didn't give a fuck what UCLA's chances were this season. Meanwhile Rikki, the bimbo, was telling her about a great place to buy name-brand skin products at a good price. Claire almost blurted out, "One does not buy one's face products at discount stores," but feared that would lead to a conversation about the pros and cons of saving ten bucks on a moisturizer.

Stuck at a table where the choices were jabber about who might make it into the upcoming Pac Ten tournament or listen to Rikki go on and on about what Allure said about eyebrow shapes this season was not Claire's idea of a fun evening. It got even worse when the guys talked about something Claire did want to join in on, because her Connecticut upbringing made her feel guilty for leaving Rikki out of the loop. Why wasn't Lawrence concerned about including his date in the conversation? It was a rhetorical question because Claire knew the answer. All Lawrence had to do to keep Rikki happy was occasionally squeeze her thigh. Why wasn't Victor concerned? Dumb question. Celebrities fulfill their obligation to be entertaining simply by showing up. Claire had all the right answers, but that didn't make the questions any easier to live with.

Victor was aware that Claire was glowering at him intermittently. Even when she smiled, it was a contemptuous smile, but he decided to ignore it. She'd done this kind of thing before and he'd given it some thought. It was the oddest thing, he'd concluded. How a woman can go from being an exotic, fascinating creature that you fall in some kind of love with, to a woman no different from countless others, complaining about the same complaints, plotting the same plots and scheming the same schemes. Where, he wanted to know, are women cool enough, secure enough, some would say inhuman enough, not to want to exert wifely control and disapproval, whether married or not?

"Anyone want dessert?" The waiter was back again, though he wasn't expecting anyone in that crowd to go for the extra calories.

"You know what I'd love?" Rikki said excitedly. "That raspberry crumble thing you have here."

Victor and Claire exchanged a look. This at least they agreed on. The bimbo's damn sweet tooth was going to keep them there for another half hour.

twenty-four

On the second day of Victor's disappearance I awoke, after a restless sleep, to record-breaking temperatures. The guest room I was staying in got morning light and the sun had already heated it up to an uncomfortable degree. It was almost nine o'clock and I felt like a sludge for sleeping so late. I threw off the covers and dragged myself over to the window, which overlooked the garage and carport. No sign of the Porsche.

I immediately opened up my laptop computer and logged onto the Internet. I checked all the entertainment news and gossip columns to see if there were any items about my boss. Sightings of him drunk at some party. A rumor of him checking into some local hotel. Any sign of life would have been good news. The big question mark was growing more ominous in spite of Alex's reassurance that everything was fine. I had to keep in mind that I'd heard Alex reassure clients that everything was fine the day before he dumped them from the agency.

Over coffee, I recapped my situation. I was temporarily

staying at my boss's house but wasn't actually doing any work for him because he had disappeared. It redefined the word "limbo." I've always been able to operate with a couple of balls in the air, but having your whole life in the air seemed a tad nerve-racking. To normal people my situation probably sounded insane, but I hadn't been normal since I was thirteen, which was when my rebelliousness and appetite for veering from the recipe first kicked in.

Problem is the flip side of being able to play it fast and loose is a low tolerance for boredom. I'd welcome the task of cooking for fifty on short notice rather than sitting at the kitchen table, watching CNN and waiting to hear a Porsche coming down the driveway. I decided if Victor didn't return by that evening, I'd return to my own house and hope that my stalker ex-boyfriend had moved on to a new obsession.

In the meantime, I made a pitcher of iced tea and took my Ross Macdonald novel out by the pool and settled in for my version of a forced vacation. Reading about Lew Archer's misadventures as a detective on a case in and around L.A. was like reading a description of the city's psychological underpinnings. Archer understood how seductive and unforgiving Southern California could be. I loved seeing L.A. through the eyes of fictitious PIs. All of them. Sam Spade. Philip Marlowe. They were excellent, observant spectators especially when it came to women. Occasionally they'd be tempted by a particularly hot dame but never to the point where they'd consider settling down and committing to a mortgage. Every so often they'd put the job on hold, if the right woman and the right moment presented itself. Details were never given but the reader was left feeling that a good time was had by all.

Whenever I came upon one of those scenes, I'd let my
imagination fly. And on that particular afternoon, it soared.
The heat was a contributing factor, as were my surround-
ings. Poolside at a beautiful estate. Total privacy. It wasn't
hard to conjure up a sexual fantasy or two. And if a Lew
Archer appeared at that moment to investigate the disappearance of my movie star boss, I might be tempted to
tempt him. Not that I was a dame, in that classic mystery-
novel way. I was a twenty-first-century girl wearing a
J.Crew bikini and Gucci sunglasses with my hair in a ponytail and a cell phone by my side.

I fell asleep forty pages into the book but I don't know for
how long. I was awakened by the ringing of my cell. The
number on caller ID was unfamiliar. I considered ignoring
it, but at the last second I answered just in case it was
Victor calling from wherever.

"Hey, pine nut? What are you doing?"

It was Shane and I immediately felt self-conscious about
sounding drowsy. Naps in midday could be construed as a
sign of depression, which unlike the heat, the pool and the
privacy was not an aphrodisiac. Doing my best to sound
alert and productive, I said, "I'm thinking about the big
salad I'm about to make."

"When are you through working for the day?"

His question stumped me. How do you answer a
straightforward question when your circumstances are anything but straight?

"It depends," I said.

"On what?"

"On when Victor gets back from his trip."

"Where is he?"

"Out of town."

"Most trips are."

At that point the conversation hit an impasse and I felt that unless I did something it would degenerate into one of those uncomfortable exchanges between two people who have enough of a connection to be talking in the first place but not enough to survive an awkward lull. So I did the very first thing that came to mind. I invited him over for lunch.

My favorite part about cooking for a guy I'm attracted to is the part where we're both in the kitchen, drinking wine, and he's watching me do something I'm good at and is impressed. The part I hate is smelling like all the food I'm cooking. Most foodies love the smell of garlic, rosemary, shallots, simmering onions and don't mind if those aromas become part of their own scent. I'm not one of them. In fact I'm going to confess something that would get me booted out of any food club. I hate garlic. HATE. I especially hate it when it's strong and you can't get the taste of it out of your mouth for, like, a day, no matter how many Altoids and BreathAsures you swallow. I prefer smelling like Kiehl's peppermint or grapefruit cleanser with a touch of Sugar-bath's lemon body lotion behind the ears and the taste of a subtle pear sorbet on my palate. However, a tasty meal obviously requires more than "eau de citrus." The ideal situation is to get the smelly part of the cooking out of the way first, take a shower and then have the guy around for the wine and the tossing of the salad—and maybe the toasting of the croutons.

I'm well aware that this attitude gets a bad rap, and the criticism can get personal. Some people have suggested to me that an unwillingness to embrace the messiness of cooking is a sign of an unwillingness to embrace the messiness of sex. NOT TRUE. Experience (and dating a few cooks) has taught me that just because a guy savors sushi does not mean that when it comes to eating pussy he's a lesbian trapped in a man's body. Just because a chef can filet a fish does not necessarily mean he has a light, skillful touch when it comes to making love. I once dated a Culinary Institute grad whose style and personality in the kitchen were so testosterone-driven and robust, I could not believe that in bed he was as bland as a Lean Cuisine frozen entrée. How one embraces food is not, contrary to widespread belief, an indicator of how one will embrace a lover. According to my world order, cooking for a guy can be a very sexy thing, only if you're feeling sexy to begin with. Which means by the time Shane arrived, lunch (pasta, with chicken, tomatoes and olives, and salad) was on the table, my hair was still wet from having just gotten out of the shower and my skin was glistening from Aveda's apricot body scrub.

Do you have friends up here for lunch often?" Shane asked. We had devoured the salad and were halfway through the pasta, and a second glass of wine.

"Never."

"Never?"

"I work here, I don't live here. Well, I do, but it's just temporary and that doesn't give me entertaining rights."

"So what would happen if Victor showed up right now?"

"I thought about that. I'd say that you dropped by because you wanted to talk to him about the movie and I said I wasn't sure when he'd be back. You asked if you could wait around for a half hour or so. And I figured since you were here and it was lunchtime . . ."

He seemed amused by my backup plan. "I come across a little lame and desperate in that story, don't you think? Waiting around someone's house, hoping they might return."

"I'm happy to go with a better lie if you've got one."

He threw out a couple more clever ones that made me laugh, but he only had half my attention. I was also thinking that the only reason I felt comfortable inviting Shane over was because I really didn't think my boss was going to show up anytime soon. That thought immediately made me nervous and uncomfortable. I was straddling optimism and pessimism and doing it badly.

"It's kind of a classic nightmare, don't you think?" Shane asked. "Owner of the house goes out of town and his employees take over the place. I think I saw a really bad movie once that had that plot."

"Not the kind of movie that you'd ever direct?" I was feeding his ego because flattery was my automatic response to any male who could inspire my lust.

"Oh, I wouldn't say that. I'm not precious about my material. I like big commercial ideas. I just like to do them a little edgier."

"How would you make that plot edgier? Sex? Drugs?"

He pushed his hair off his face, a gesture that has as much to do with his rock 'n' roll style as it did with an adorable boyishness. "Well, to begin with I'd have a scene

that involved a man and a woman out by a pool on an unseasonably hot spring day."

What was I supposed to do? Say no? Ignore the invitation? Pretend that line wasn't meant to be an invitation? This was a guy who had a Michael Hutchence
mystique and I was a woman whose whole life was in limbo.
It was a match made for a hot afternoon interlude up in an
L.A. canyon.

We both knew it was a done deal from the second we got
up from the table, but we let it play out in gradual steps.
Step one: Lying by the pool in bathing suits (well, he was
wearing Dolce & Gabbana boxers) and finishing off the
remainder of the bottle of wine. Step two: Sharing the same
lounge chair under the pretense of him putting what was
left of the sunblock on my shoulders (a move that was so
cliché we both should have been embarrassed by the obvi-
ousness of it but weren't). Step three: The first kiss that got
things going—fast. Step four: Dolce underwear and bikini
bottoms get tossed, with the bikini landing in the pool. Step
five: He fulfills my Michael Hutchence fantasy, which is to
say Shane knew how to please. As Elizabeth West and I
have joked, there are penetrators and there are inhabitors.
Some guys think fucking is about penetration. That's it. As
opposed to the ones who stick around for a while and make
sure, like any good guest, that while they're visiting, they're
responsive, sensitive and exciting.

If you're thinking this was brave or reckless of me, considering there was the outside chance that Victor could show
up at any moment, I have to admit that there was an ex-

tremely low risk of getting caught. The pool area was not visible from the driveway. I would hear a car approaching a good fifteen seconds before it reached the garage. No one else was working at the house that afternoon, and though the gardeners had access to the grounds, this wasn't one of their workdays.

I also had to go for it because I knew that sex with Shane would temporarily block out the ominous thoughts that I'd woken up with on this, the second day of my boss's disappearance. I was in no rush to reenter reality. Nor, judging by his stamina, was Shane. Lucky me. Well, maybe not that lucky because my cell phone started ringing. I ignored it. It stopped. It started again. I ignored it again. It stopped. It started again. My choice was to answer it or throw it into the pool.

I picked it up. Incoming call from an area code I didn't even recognize. If it was my ex-boyfriend stalker, I swear I would have threatened him with a restraining order. It was one thing to scare me away from living in my own house; it was another to interrupt my rare trip to fantasyland.

"What?" I said.

"Nice hello you got going there." It was Victor.

"Oh my God. Where are you?"

"Where are you? Are you in your car? Are you on the 405 heading to the airport?" He laughed.

At least he was alive and laughing. "Am I supposed to be?" For a second I panicked, worried that I'd somehow missed a message and was about to get into trouble.

Out of what I assume was politeness, Shane made a move to get off me but I rubbed his lower back with my free hand to keep him there.

"You are now," Victor replied. I could hear a lot of noise in the background.

"Are you at Disneyland?" It was the most absurd guess I could think of.

"Close. Vegas. The Bellagio. See you when you get here."

He hung up before I could get any more information, and Shane put his mouth on mine before I could give any. My sexy lunch date didn't seem to care who called me or why, or maybe he cared but his dick didn't. And I have to say I loved him for that.

ater, as he was putting his clothes back on, I imagined what it would be like to be able to hang out leisurely with Shane, maybe go to a movie together. A moment later this thought popped into my head. I'd never, in all the Ross Macdonald books I'd read, ever come across a scene in which Lew Archer gets to go to a movie—unless of course he's tailing a suspect.

I was about to ask Shane if he'd ever read a mystery novel in which the detective got to have any fun, but stopped because at that moment he seemed deeply concerned about something. He was looking around as if there might be someone hiding in the bushes.

"What's the matter?"

Shane looked over to the small pool house as he zipped up his pants. "Victor doesn't have security cameras around here, does he?"

"Caught on tape," I said.

He froze as if someone had put a gun to his back.

"Just kidding."

twenty-five

The Hummer passed through the flats of Beverly Hills toward Sunset. Very little had been said since Mr. Famous and Claire had left the restaurant. The buzz from the alcohol they'd consumed was wearing off and neither one of them was in very good spirits. It was not the time to bring up any topic that required too much thought or any emotion, but Claire couldn't help herself.

"Are we going to take that trip to France?"

Mr. F slowed down at a stop sign and then hit the accelerator. "I don't know."

Claire persisted. "I thought we made plans."

"Plans? We made plans?"

"Well, that's what it's called when you discuss going to the Paris Open for the semifinal and final matches."

"No, I think that's called a discussion. Plans are when you've got a plane reservation and an ETA." He was too tired for this and it bothered him that he was too tired. It was only eleven o'clock. It seemed not that long ago he'd just be starting the night at this hour. Being slowed down by age was not something he was ready to deal with. He was only forty-six. Better to think he was being slowed down by Claire.

The Hummer came to a complete stop at the intersection in front of the Beverly Hills Hotel. A streetlight illuminated Mr. F's face. Claire was struck by how lost in his own thoughts he appeared. As if she weren't even there. At that very moment she realized that she was investing her time and energy in a man who was comfortable being alone with his thoughts. A man who could handle solitude. It usually worked the other way. Most actors and actresses she knew preferred company because life on the set had become their norm. When she first met Mr. F, at a party, he had a posse of buddies with him, including the stunt coordinator from his last flick and his boxing coach. Her first impression of him was that he traveled in a pack. *That* she could handle. But there was something about how easily he was drifting away from her at that moment that woke her to the truth of her situation. He didn't need her the way she needed him and consequently she had less power here than she'd thought.

"You don't get plane reservations until you make a plan to get them." Claire did her best not to broadcast her exasperation but her voice was approaching screech levels. "The plan comes first, the reservations come second."

"It's four months away," Mr. F said. "Who knows what can happen between now and then."

She took that to mean who knew where they'd be—as a couple—four months from now. The fact that he was so iffy about their relationship triggered her rage as the

Hummer cruised up Benedict Canyon. Mr. F was unaware that her silence spelled trouble. All he was thinking about was whether or not he should drop Claire off at her house or if they should continue to his place as they'd discussed (she would say planned) earlier in the day.

When they got as far up the road as Hutton, a car turning off that side street got in front of them, causing Mr. F to drop into second gear.

"Who the fuck drives the speed limit up here," he said as he made a failed attempt to pass the slow-moving Honda.

Claire was glad at his flash of temper. It may not justify the love she still felt for this man, but it helped justify her anger.

twenty-six

Though the flight to Vegas is often a turbulent one, and my claustrophobia doesn't help, those were not the main reasons I chose to drive. I did it because I've always done my best thinking in the car and I needed to mull over a few thousand things before dealing with whatever was waiting for me in Sin City. There was the big issue of what I was doing with my life. There was the issue of sex with Shane. Hard not to think about that, seeing as it was the first time I'd ever had such an intense orgasm *while* giving a blow job.

Wanting to savor and save that memory for later, I moved on to more superficial concerns. I thought about whether I should toss my J.Crew bathing suits and order something sexier from the Victoria's Secret catalog. I also thought about how nice it was to simply be on the road, in transit, moving toward a destination I didn't dread.

Though I knew that my boss assumed I'd get to Vegas ASAP, when you factored in the time it'd take to book a flight (assuming you could get one leaving soon) and arrive

at the airport (forty-five minutes away) at least an hour before departure time, driving would only take a couple of
hours more and would be a lot less stressful. Plus, I loved
being in my car. Probably because it was the only big thing
that I owned and being in it made me feel safe and secure.
I could either arrive in Vegas stressed out and ragged from
air travel, or secure and full of ideas from my meditative
drive. No contest.

Once I got out of inner-city traffic and crossed the
county line, I found my groove and got into my favorite mental zone, the one that allowed my mind to free-
associate while never losing my focus on the road. I came
to the conclusion that a Victoria's Secret bathing suit with
underwire push-up bra top in black was the way to go. I also
spent time thinking about why I was being called to Vegas.
Certainly not to whip up an egg-white omelette. It was one
thing to intrude on the cooking staff of a small new England inn, another to crash the kitchen at the Bellagio. The
more I thought about it, the more confused I became. It was
possible there was no specific reason. It was very, very possible Victor could have been operating on a whim. He might
have been in the mood to talk to me at that moment but
maybe by the time I arrived the whim would be long gone
and my presence would be viewed as an intrusion. I've seen
Hollywood heavyweights pull this kind of thing even when
they're not going through a crack-up. Then again, maybe
Victor really did need me. Was I his buffer from the real
world or his link to it? Or neither?

I decided to call and ask him outright what it was I was

coming there to do. I pulled off the freeway into a gas station. While my oil and tires were being checked (an L.A. psychic had told me I should check my back tires often), I reached for my cell phone but came up empty-handed. Of course it wasn't there. It was all coming back to me. I'd left it under the lounge chair, out by the pool. I hated not having my phone with me. I thought of all the calls I'd miss as if they were missed opportunities, not missed headaches, though that was more likely. Being without my Nokia also made me feel vulnerable. I'd have to get out of my womb of a car and find a public phone, which was no easy thing since cells have taken over the world.

The attendant directed me to the corner of the station's mini mart, where I found one in working order. It wasn't until I heard the dial tone that I realized I didn't know how to reach Victor. He wouldn't be registered under his real name. Big celebrities rarely do that, and I knew that Victor never did because his heroic film roles attracted a lot of overly enthusiastic fans.

When I got through to the hotel, I tried asking for him under his real name, just in case his flip-out, or whatever you want to call it, had changed his traveling pattern. A guy at the front desk informed me that there was no guest registered under that name. I tried Victor's brother's name. Nope. I didn't know the name of the character in the book *Skate* but I did ask for a Victor Skate. Movie stars get into a lot of cutesy things when they go for an alias. Not this time. I could tell the front desk guy was losing patience with me.

"Look," I said, "I know you're probably thinking I'm some weirdo who heard Victor is in Vegas and now I'm trying to track him down, but that's not the case. I work for him. He's expecting me."

"We have no one registered under any of those names," the man repeated.

"Can I leave a message for him then?"

"You can't leave a message for a guest who isn't registered at this hotel."

"Okay, okay," I said, almost ready to accept defeat. "Let me just try one more thing. Do you have a Mr. Famous registered there? No first name. Just Mr. Famous."

"Hold on," the man replied, a little less snippy.

While I waited, I watched a couple fill up their Honda Accord at self-serve. While the man worked the pump, the woman wiped their windshield. They struck me as a couple who'd been married for a while and went about their designated tasks like a well-coordinated unit. It was a form of harmonious consensus that was as far outside my life experience as Siegfried and Roy.

When the guy at the front desk got back on the line he made no attempt to extend any Bellagio hospitality.

"I'll ring through," he said.

"Thanks." Wow, I thought. Wow. I loved that Victor was using the nickname I gave him as his alias. It felt as good as if I'd come up with a line that he'd ad-libbed in a movie, which then became part of the pop culture. A "make my day" kind of line. A little celebrity approval goes a long away—even for a girl who prides herself on being appropriately jaded about those kinds of things.

"Are you here?" Victor's voice was forceful without being demanding.

"Halfway."

"I'll have a car waiting for you at the airport."

"You will? That's so sweet but you don't need to. I'm driving."

"What's with you?" He was teasing me now.

"It just worked out to be the easiest way to go. I'll be there in another couple of hours."

"We'll be waiting for you."

We'll? Who else was there? I was afraid to ask.

"Okay then," I said, ready to hang up until I realized that I'd almost forgotten the whole point of the call. A pronoun like "we" can do that. Especially when it's put out there and left dangling. A dangling pronoun can drive me nuts.

"Wait," I said as he started to sign off. "I was wondering, why am I coming to Vegas?"

"Why?"

"Yeah, why?"

"Because you work for me."

"I get that part, but . . ." I didn't finish because I suddenly realized what a moron I was. If these big, fancy suites have pools and Jacuzzis and even, I'm told—in those reserved for major players—a putting green or a driving range, of course they have a kitchen. Maybe two. I was about to cover my moronic mistake by adding, I just want to know if you need me to pick up any groceries, but he cut me off.

"And because I think better with you in the room."

It was the nicest thing anyone had said to me in a really long time.

. . .

That phone call put me in the best mood. I was psyched for the second half of the trip and decided to pick up a few snacks at the tiny food mart next to the gas station. They'd crammed a little bit of everything into that small space. There were the usual chips, soda and candy. You could also buy condoms, greeting cards and hair accessories. I wasn't tempted by anything until I saw the tabloids displayed next to the register. Guess who got a cover headline? VICTOR MASON FINDS NEW LOVE IN A CAPE COD HIDEAWAY. There was a small snapshot of Victor taken at some social gathering juxtaposed with a shot of Layla from some Hollywood party. The inside story was a two-page deal. There were enough details to point to Layla, or her publicist, as the unnamed source. Fucking fame chasers. They were turning Hollywood from a dream factory into, well . . . just a factory. Worse was the spin on the details. It was all about how the happy couple was madly in love and how they were already looking for a project to work on together. Bullshit. Victor hadn't even mentioned Layla's name since we got on the plane at Logan Airport. I wondered if I should show him the article. What if he found it amusing? What if it inspired him to pick up the phone and call her? So what? Let him. If he wanted to spend time with women who were the equivalent of a third rail on a high-voltage subway track that was his problem. Not mine. Unless . . . the "we" he'd dangled referred to him and Layla. Oh great. Was I being summoned to make them breakfast in bed? It didn't seem likely but I couldn't rule it out. If I've learned anything from being a Hollywood chef, it's that people with lots of options usually take a lot of them.

I've always considered L.A. more of a gambler's mecca than Vegas. People bet their money in the casinos. People wager everything in tinseltown. For the really high rollers the motto could be "Win or die." They're the ones who come to town willing to sacrifice and endure whatever it takes to get a place at Hollywood's head table. You can end up living so far out on a limb, the tree you climbed to get there is in another zip code. At first it can be exhilarating, until the credit cards max out and you end up living on a friend's couch. Of course you spin it by saying something like, "Do you know how difficult it is to find a great house in L.A.?" You juggle tax payments to the IRS, loan payments to City National Bank and your monthly membership fees at the gym. You do it not only because you believe you have a shot at winning, but because in order to get out on that limb in the first place you had to let go of any desire for any other kind of life. In Vegas you can lose your nest egg. In Hollywood you can lose your nest egg, your nest and your entire family tree. High rollers can't go home again. Not if they lose. Not even if they win. Victor was proof of that. The chances that people in Hollywood take, against odds that only a fool in Vegas would play, are scarier than any Hitchcock thriller.

I found him at the slot machines, wearing his usual camouflage: hat, wraparound Italian sunglasses, leather racecar jacket zipped up. But what made Victor's disguise so effective that at first glance I didn't even recognize him was the older man he was standing next to. He was definitely not an L.A. person. His boxy, wrinkled gray suit hung over his tall bony frame. That, along with his sharp angular features, made him look like an underfed horse. He peered out at me through thick, black square-framed glasses that reminded me of my seventh-grade math teacher. When I walked up to them, he was pocketing his winnings.

"Hi," I said.

Victor gave me a hug. "Good timing. We're done here."

The older guy smiled at me as if I were his good luck charm. Was this the other half of Victor's "we"?

"Slots?" I asked, with the same incredulity that I'd have if I'd stumbled upon Victor eating Chicken McNuggets.

"It relaxes Earl," Victor explained.

"This relaxes you, Earl?"

"Yes it does, Lucinda."

"You know my name? What else do you know?"

"He knows everything," Victor exclaimed.

"Everything? Really, Earl? Then maybe you can tell me why I always sneeze more than once but never hiccup more than six times in a row?"

It was a poorly conceived stab at being cute, but Earl looked like he was straining to come up with an actual answer. Victor just kept going, pumping out the praise because he was having too much fun to stop. "And get this. Guess what Earl used to do when he was younger."

"Private detective?" I guessed, basing my answer on the "he knows everything" cue.

"He used to drive a moving van. Isn't that great?"

Earl looked uncomfortable with the attention. "Moved a lot of people," he admitted.

"Congratulations." I had no idea what else to say and no curiosity about his adventures on the road.

"I've had a good life for someone who's not lucky."

"What do you call that?" I asked, looking at his slot winnings.

"Perseverance."

The blanks were filled in over a dinner of steak, baked potatoes and salad. My boss was back on carbs and Earl and I were right there with him. It was close to midnight but the dining room was buzzing. Victor had taken off his hat and glasses, and even though we took a booth in a back corner, the word was out that he was in the house. Every ten minutes or so another fan would politely interrupt to ask for an autograph. It was during these interactions that I picked up the most information.

Victor scribbled his name on a menu for a woman who, if described as an aging hottie, would take it as a compliment. "Earl is the one you should be getting an autograph from," he said.

She scrutinized Earl from head to toe. "And why should I want your autograph, Earl?"

"You got me," he replied.

Victor got a kick out of Earl's shyness or humility or whatever it was. "Because," Victor explained, "Earl wrote one of the all-time great books."

"As good as the Bible or *Titanic*?"

"*Titanic* wasn't a book," Earl said softly.

"Felt like one," the woman answered. "So what's the name of Earl's great book?"

"*Skate,*" Victor said.

"*Skate,*" she repeated. And then sticking out her ample chest and putting her hands on her hips, she looked right at Victor and suggestively added, "I like to skate. I like to do a lot of physical things. I'm very athletic."

"Is that right?" Victor said, trying to be nice, but this Vegas broad wouldn't have been his type at twenty. With another couple of decades on her and that crass come-on, she was borderline repulsive. Problem was Victor's new incarnation as "one of the people" made it difficult for him to move her out. Thank God the waiter chose that moment to clear the plates and I took that opportunity to redirect traffic.

"Thanks for stopping by," I said. "Enjoy the rest of your night."

She glared at me and then looked over to Victor, but he was engaged in a conversation with Earl. She swung her gaze back to me as if it were all my fault.

"What are you, his girlfriend?"

"No. Just a girl."

Over dessert, I got to ask a few of my own questions. The answers were yes and yes. Earl had optioned the book to Claire, who had brought it to Daniel over at Next Wave Films and he gave her a deal to develop it. Nodding in Victor's direction, he admitted he regretted it, "because no one gets my book like this guy does, but how was I supposed to know I'd be meeting up with him."

"Did you accidentally meet?"

Victor finished the last bite of his chocolate cake. "I tracked Earl down in Maine and sent him a ticket to meet me in Vegas."

"So what's the plan now?" I assumed there was some plan to get the rights to the book back from Claire.

"I go back east first thing tomorrow morning," Earl replied.

I looked to Victor. "And what about the book, the option and all of that?"

"As important as that is, it's not important," he said.

Oh Christ, I thought. Was he going to start talking in Buddhist koans? "What is important?"

"Alignment," he said.

My first thought was tires but I guessed he was probably talking about something a little more spiritual.

"Besides, Earl signed the deal."

"I think I should send those cocksuckers their money back and tell them to fuck off," Earl laughed, suddenly not so shy or humble.

"We're talking Hollywood, the land of a million litigators," I said. "They just might end up costing you money and keeping your book."

Living up to his reputation as a man who knows everything or can make it sound as if he's in on something you're not, he just smiled and said, "I take pride in never reading the small print."

After Earl left, Victor and I stayed put for one more drink. He apologized for making me come all the way to Vegas for no good reason. I considered reminding him that he thinks better with me in the room. I considered saying, Don't take my favorite compliment and turn it into no good reason. Instead, I stirred my drink with my finger and said, "I enjoyed the drive."

"When I called you," he continued, "I thought I'd be sticking around here for a while, but now I'm thinking I need to get back to L.A."

"It'll be nice to have you home," I said, as if he and I shared a home. As if I wasn't just an employee who had been given temporary shelter in what used to be the maid's room.

"Funny how things happen," he said.

I had no idea what he was talking about, which was happening more and more lately. Didn't matter. So what if he jumped from one thing to the next? So what if I didn't have all the data. Sometimes you have to forfeit information to stay in the flow of a certain mood. Small sacrifice because it was such a great mood. It was a salad of comfort and stimulation, tossed with an alcohol and sugar dressing. I'd drive all night to get to this.

"You got that right," I said, which encouraged him to ramble about the various things he'd been thinking about, which included the importance of good sportsmanship, a new CD by a group called the Supreme Beings of Leisure and Norman Vincent Peale's belief that attitude is more important than fact. I suspected Earl had inspired some of this but the source didn't matter. What counted was that sitting there talking to Victor made me feel like a winner. How could I not feel good about a day that included afternoon poolside sex with Shane and a midnight chat with my slightly loony but always interesting boss. Not to mention an excellently cooked New York steak. I felt as if I'd just gotten a triple match at the slots. If the conversation wasn't so damned intriguing, I think I would have tried my luck at blackjack. I felt so sure of myself and my prospects that I confessed the Shane incident, and thankfully, my luck held. No lectures from the boss. He looked a little bewildered but I couldn't decide if that was because he couldn't see Shane with a girl like me or couldn't see me with a guy like Shane. He refrained from commentary but did revert to one of his favorite games.

"You might want to ask yourself why you're afraid to fly."

Was he talking planes or relationships? "Claustrophobic," I said.

"You've been traveling with the wrong people."

It was a comment worthy of Dr. Davenport and I told him so.

"Nothing against *the great doc,*" he said, "but you might want to consider he's one of the wrong people."

"You got someone better."

"Yeah," he laughed. "Earl."

At that moment it seemed like a pretty decent idea and we clinked glasses over it. I know I was supposed to be the sane one and he was the one having a crack-up, but I was beginning to feel as if in his own haphazard way he was pushing through some blocks and gaining yardage, while I was still stuck on my line of scrimmage. And because I felt I was on a roll, this hit me as the good news. A wake-up call. "Hey dummy, you've been misdiagnosed as relatively sane when you're positively stuck. Fix it." And at that moment I swore to myself I would and clinked glasses again for more good luck, not knowing that I'd already run out. A voice that annoyed me even when it wasn't crashing my party grounded my flight of fancy.

"Hi, baby," Layla said, before planting a big kiss on Victor. She was wearing a lacy gold top, tight black pants and visible La Perla thong underwear. When she leaned over the table to get to Victor, her butt was practically in my face and the tag was showing.

"Don't mind us," she said.

"Do I have a choice?" I mumbled.

She didn't reply but she did sit down, on his side of the table, and posed, looking at him adoringly. Really posed, to the point where I looked around, expecting to see a photographer from Page Six.

"Hungry?" Victor asked her.

That's when I relaxed. It's been my experience that if the first thing a guy says when you show up at his table and kiss him is "Hungry?" it's not a good sign. Hungry is something you say to stall for time. Hungry is something you say to be polite. Hungry is something you say to your child who's just come in after playing soccer for two hours. It is not something you say to a lover who has just arrived in Vegas to be with you. If I were Layla, I'd be hearing alarm bells, but she evidently heard nothing.

"I'd love a drink," she said, helping herself to a sip of his.

"Finish it," he said. "I'm through for the night."

That did set off an alarm. A small one. "You're through for the night? I just got here."

"You girls should go out, have some fun." He peeled ten hundreds out of a roll in his pocket and put them on the table.

Now that alarm was ringing loud. Four-alarm fire, judging by the smoke that was practically coming out of Layla's ears. She stood up.

"Fuck you, Victor. Fuck you."

I'd never been around Victor in one of these situations before but I've been told that he can be intimidating. I'd also seen his movie *Velocity*, where he played a race car driver who could bring even the toughest diva bitch to her knees with just a look. I knew he had it in him. But, whether out of compassion or fatigue, he kept that character under wraps.

"If I'd have known you were coming," he said calmly.

She cut him off. "You knew I was coming."

"No. You said you were thinking of coming to Vegas."

"That's right. And you said, sounds good."

I so badly wanted to jump in because I knew exactly what was happening. In addition to being a chef, and a fledgling detective, maybe my job also required some of Dr. Phil's skills. I wanted to say, STOP. Okay, guys, let me explain. Saying you're thinking of coming to Vegas does not mean that if you show up without another call confirming your arrival, you can reasonably expect the person you're visiting to be on your schedule. Secondly, saying "sounds good," though not the same as saying I want you to come, can lead a person into thinking they'd be welcomed. And then turning directly to Victor, I'd say, And let me give you a little tip about women. When they put on their most expensive La Perlas (those thong undies cost two hundred dollars)—maybe even buy them especially for the occasion—they expect to get fucked. And if you pass on the sex, it can lead to short-term rage or long-term hatred. It's a little too close to every girl's nightmare—being all decked out in your Vera Wang gown and left stranded at the altar.

I didn't have the guts to jump in and I certainly wasn't getting any invitations. Victor pulled Layla off to a quiet corner for a private chat. Anyone could see they were having a fight. I didn't know what to do, so I just smiled at the busboy and waiters who walked by as if to say, Everything's fine. No problem. I kept that up for another five minutes till Layla returned solo.

"Fuck him. Fuck him. Fuck him," she said.

The thousand dollars was still on the table. She lit a match and held it up to a C-note. As it started to burn, she blew it out. "Fuck him."

Then she gathered up the money and looked at me for the first time since she arrived. "There's a party at the Hard Rock. Wanna come?"

twenty-seven

These girls can't travel alone. I know the deal. They need backup. Yeah, like a lot has changed since they were in high school. Girls like Layla don't want to show up—can't show up—at a party without a sidekick, or even better, an entourage. I had no interest in being part of her posse—a concept I'm sure she'd find perplexing. People like Layla look at people like me and assume it's a step up for us to be hanging with them. She still thinks she's an "It" girl, even though, at twenty-eight, she's too old to be one. Too bad her brain hasn't caught up with her chronology.

The reason I said yes to her party invitation was because talking to Victor got me all revved up. Vegas was cranking me up even further. It's such a surreal atmosphere, I felt bizarre opting for something as normal as sleep when it was only a little after midnight. Most of all I said yes because when I called Victor's room, he had a Do Not Disturb on his phone. It felt like a slammed door in my face, and

I knew that if I didn't get lost in distractions, I'd bet all my cash and lose big. Can't win when you're feeling like a loser. Hollywood teaches you that.

The party at the Hard Rock Hotel was for someone's birthday. I was introduced to the Birthday Boy but it was so fucking loud I couldn't catch the name. The whole place was too loud for me. Music everywhere you went and these revelers were loud to begin with. Layla practically screamed hello at every familiar face she ran into. She was also a chain-smoker. I love secondhand smoke but this girl blew it in your eyes. She appeared completely unaware of her bad habits and I had to wonder how she even rated a "sounds good" from Victor. What sounded good about this tornado blowing in? It would be easy to jump to the assumption that it was all about sex. But not only could I read my boss's mood based on where he put his car keys when he came home, I could also read his attraction to women based on his appetite "the morning after." If the sex wasn't great, he craved carbs. If the sex was hot, all he wanted was protein. The morning after he first hooked up with Layla, he made me stop at a bakery on our way to Logan Airport. He bought jelly doughnuts. That tells you everything.

Except it doesn't explain why he didn't discourage Layla from coming to Vegas in the first place. The only explanation I could come up with was that in his efforts to get in touch with his real self, he was experimenting with different behaviors. It's a little like going through boxes of your old stuff in an attic or storage room. If you come across a hat you used to wear, you might want to try it on to see if it still fits. Maybe Victor was trying on the laissez-faire hat, which when you think about it is the exact opposite of what action heroes do. Action heroes act. They make things happen. They make things happen their way. In all honesty, I have to say I was beginning to miss the old persona. Davenport may have been correct in suggesting that if Victor was going to survive in Hollywood, or anyplace else, he was going to have to reconnect to his real self. I just hoped that the real Victor had more testosterone than the guy who came to Vegas and called it quits at midnight.

I watched Layla get more and more drunk and come on to the Birthday Boy, who was juggling a few other women. I had a glass and a half of champagne and two Excedrin, which come packed with caffeine, so I was speeding. Ideas were flying in and out of my head, which, at the time, seemed insightful. After the second glass of champagne, some of them seemed borderline brilliant. I didn't mind that Layla only paid attention to me if there was a slight lull in her efforts to get attention elsewhere. I was watching her as if she were the subject of a documentary called Party Girl, Interrupted. There was a compulsiveness and panic to Layla's come-on that made for compelling viewing. If that sounds cold, what was I supposed to do? Intervene? You try doing an intervention on a starlet you hardly know in the middle of a party at the Hard Rock Hotel.

So I just watched as she went through the seven steps to a spiritual lapse. That's the description I came up with when I was buzzed enough to think it was, if not brilliant, at least clever.

The first step was acting inappropriately provocative. Unzipping her pants and pulling them halfway down so Birthday Boy could see her tattoo was too much information in a public place. Of course he checked her out but then almost immediately turned his attention to one of the other girls he was juggling. This prompted Layla to move to the second step: punishing him for his lack of enthusiasm by flirting with one of his friends. Though withholding is a tried-and-true technique, you've got to choose your moment. Withholding when the guy's not trying to hold on is an exercise in frustration and can lead to a revenge fuck, which is never, ever a good idea. Layla didn't take it that far because she wasn't clueless and at that point wasn't too inebriated to recognize a change in tactics was necessary.

So she moved on to step three, which called for reeling the Birthday Boy back in with a secret. The only reason I know this is because she confided in him while standing next to me at the end of the bar and speaking louder than she should, even with the sound system blasting Aerosmith. I got the gist of it because she kept repeating, "I know he's a big movie star and all and no one can know I've been seeing him." It was classic Party Girl, Interrupted behavior. Lure Birthday Boy into what was left of her web by creating a dramatic triangle involving herself, him and a macho celebrity, whom he probably admired. It'd be the equivalent of saying to a twenty-four-year-old who grew up obsessed with comic book heroes, I'm choosing you over Spider-Man, and then upping the drama by making it all undercover and covert. It's a workable strategy as long as you have credibility. When you start stumbling over your words and tugging on Birthday Boy's sleeve, you run the risk of having him think you're totally bonkers. The look on Birthday Boy's face as he listened to Layla's "confession" was pained, as if he'd just had a root canal and the anesthesia was wearing off. I couldn't hear what his reply to all this was but after talking for another five minutes, he gave Layla a quick kiss and was back to working the room.

It was a half hour before she found the moment to make the move that qualified as step four. When she spotted a guy who worked for *US Weekly*, she dashed up to him, grabbed his arm and whispered something in his ear. He smiled gleefully. She was either offering to blow him or giving him a good piece of gossip. Her mission accomplished, and with no other targets in sight, she rejoined me at the bar.

"I did the best I could to contain the situation," she said. Only it came out *sisuation*.

"What situation?"

"The situation. Me. Victor. Both in the same city. Spotted together at the Bellagio. Hello? People could speculate. Plus, I'm a guest at a birthday party for one of Hollywood's up-and-comers. Hello?" She put her hands together to make a triangle, as if I needed a visual aid.

"Are you dating the guest of honor?" If he was an up-and-comer, he wasn't on my radar.

"I can't talk about it," she said, "but of course that journalist from *US Weekly* says we are." She threw her arms up in a dramatic gesture that I think was supposed to mean, What can you do with these journalists? "I told him if he's going to run an item on it, quote me as saying, 'Well, you do know that the triangle is the strongest geometric shape.'" She laughed. "My publicist told me that if you give them a funny quote, they don't go nasty/bitchy on you."

That was her idea of containment. It was one step away from slipping the journalist five hundred to guarantee the non-item ran.

The fifth step toward her spiritual lapse came when she repeated all of this to the Birthday Boy, leaving out the quote and in its place inserting a plea for why the two of them had to stand together against all the sleazy reporters in the world. The us-against-the-world ploy is another very workable trick and can often accelerate a relationship, but only if you share a common enemy and the guy wants you on his team. Birthday Boy had invited the journalist there so he probably wanted to be written up, but not in an item with Layla, who was one sip away from sloppy drunk.

I watched the guy step out of range so he wouldn't be photographed with her. When he propped her up against the bar and moved on, she turned to me and said, "He's such a gentleman." Wrong caption for that would-be snapshot. She was now at the sixth step, which is very slippery, dangerous ground. She was ignoring the information and letting her ego talk her into a "sisuation" that didn't exist.

It was only a matter of time—in this case twenty minutes or so—before Layla realized her gentleman was off in a corner being less than gentlemanly with a gorgeous girl in a leather mini. Hello, seventh step: anger and revenge.

Layla exploded, and before I could attempt to calm her down, she marched over to the entwined couple, grabbed the girl in the mini's arm to get her attention and screamed, "He's a fag." Only people in the immediate vicinity heard Layla, thanks to the volume on a cut from an old Mötley Crüe album, and they either laughed or ignored her. Birthday Boy and his babe just kept on kissing.

She cried in the taxi on the way back to the Bellagio. She knew she'd had a spiritual lapse—make that spiritual crash—which is why I was still hanging around. If she'd acted like the victim I would have insisted on separate cabs. She knew she'd fucked up, and I'd fucked up too many times myself not to have a little sympathy. She divulged a few things on that ride that even made me feel a little protective. I found out that she was struggling to get by. There was no rich daddy, no rich lover, boyfriend or ex to help her out. In fact, her family in Portland, Oregon, counted on her to bail them out. She was a high-stakes player with a lot to lose. I felt a kinship to her plight, if not to her personality. I know there are people who would say if you can't afford to lose, don't play at a high-stakes table. But I say if you can afford to lose, the stakes aren't all that high. Don't misunderstand me. I'm not an excitement junkie. I don't need to have the possibility of total annihilation to make me feel alive. I'd prefer to have a big fat financial cushion. All I'm saying is that those of us who don't have a safety net and still go for a life that offers no security can't help but feel some kind of connection to each other. Layla had bad judgment and she was a bad drunk but she lived out on the same limb I did and it inspired some neighborly sentiments.

"It's just been one of those kinds of night," I said. "Don't worry about it. We all have them."

"That's sweet. It's crap but it's sweet."

"It's crap? Where'd that come from?"

"You wouldn't be hanging around me for five minutes if I wasn't part of Victor's life. It's situational kindness. I'm not saying don't do it. But come on."

She may have been down and out but she was still able to get to the root of my charity in record time. I knew she was right because all I could say in rebuttal was, "Funny how we can talk ourselves in or out of things."

"You're talking to the queen," she said.

When we got to the hotel we discovered that Victor had checked out. He'd left no note but had paid for a room for each of us for one night. I was ready to get some sleep, but Layla was reluctant to be alone.

"If I go to sleep feeling this bad, there's no chance I'll wake up feeling better," she said. Her tears and disappointment had sobered her up some and I figured a coffee wouldn't hurt. I figured a half hour maximum. I ordered decaf and tried to move the conversation on to subjects that wouldn't encourage bad dreams. For her or me. Clothes. Jewelry designers. The thin-crust pizza at Orso. I can't say that she perked up much but she wasn't crying. When she got up to go to the ladies' room, I used her phone to check my messages in case Victor had left one on my cell phone. I had seven new ones. I never have seven new messages. I'm not that popular. The first one was from Shane. I hadn't expected him to call until the next day, but there he was checking in at six P.M., mere hours after our erotic interlude in Victor's backyard. He just wanted to tell me I was the first good surprise he'd had in months and he hoped we could get together again. That certainly perked me up, which was why the following calls felt like an ambush. There I was with a big stupid happy smile on my face, never expecting to get hit by six bullets. That's what it felt like to hear the remaining messages. All of them the full voice-mail length of time—three minutes. All of them the first three minutes of the same cacophonous heavy metal hate song. I couldn't dismiss this as some crank caller. I knew it was my stalker. Layla had returned in time for the last three messages and watched me grow more and more horrified.

"What's wrong?"

"I can't talk about it," I said. I snapped the phone shut but couldn't shut down the image of Matt at some phone booth getting off on rewinding the cassette. Stop, I told myself. You cannot let your mind go there. I couldn't handle being alone in a strange hotel room in Vegas, scared awake by my nightmares.

"How tired are you?" I asked Layla.

"I'm the one drinking caffeine," she replied.

"Up for a crazy idea?"

"How crazy?"

"Let's go back to the party at the Hard Rock."

"Let's not."

"No, wait, listen. We go back there and dance. You and me. We'll ignore everyone else." Only exercise could purge my anxiety and I wasn't about to get on a treadmill.

I was about to explain this to her when she said, "Yes. Okay. Only if we ignore everyone else. Is that a deal? It'll be like we're on a date and are madly in love. Minus the public display of affection." She thought a minute. "Or not," she said as she very affectionately rubbed my arm.

We ended up dancing till five in the morning. Sometimes when you're on the losing side of a high-stakes game, the most important thing you can do is prove to yourself and whoever might be watching that bad dice and all, you're still shaking it up on the dance floor.

twenty-eight

He would have dropped Claire off if he could have figured out a way to do it without a war. He was tired. They'd already fucked that afternoon. He was in no mood to talk. It was possible she felt the same way. But he knew she expected to spend the night at his place and clearly Claire wasn't a very flexible girl when it came to plans. She jokingly blamed it on her astrological sign— Virgo—and her WASP heritage. In the past he'd indulged her on this issue, but lately he had no patience for her in-flexibility. Worse, it bored him. Were his choices boredom or a fight? How did it come to this? He was still pondering the question, even after the decision was made.

"So, Mr. Famous," Claire said mockingly as she stepped out of his bathroom naked. He was lying on the bed, the TV remote in his hand. "Trying to find one of your movies?"

He upped the volume on CNN. A weak comeback by his standards and he was a little disappointed in himself for being so passive.

Claire posed at the end of the bed. "It's insulting to ignore your girlfriend when she's standing naked in front of you."

He cringed at the word "girlfriend" but did glance up at her. "Lovely," he said and went back to watching the news.

By anybody's standards his nonchalance was more hostile than passive. Claire picked up on it immediately. It had taken her many years to gain the confidence to strut around naked in a room that didn't have a dimmer on every lighting fixture, many years of jogging, Pilates classes and two lipo surgeries. I've turned into an L.A. bimbo for this guy, she thought. And for what?

At that moment a CNN anchor segued to an item from the tennis world. The lid was off the Paris box once again.

"So what's it going to be, Victor?"

Claire's tone was modulated and reasonable, but there was no mistaking the escalation in her intensity. This was her Virgo-esque, WASP way of declaring war.

twenty-nine

My job description changed again. Only in Hollywood can a chef end up as a development executive overnight. When I got back to L.A. from Vegas, Victor informed me that I'd be coming to a meeting he'd scheduled with Daniel, Claire's new boyfriend, the head of the studio who financed *Last Standing* and now the owner of the option on *Skate*. At first I thought he wanted me to chauffeur him there, but when he handed me the book *Skate* and said I should make notes on how it could best be adapted to a film, I realized we were on new ground. Both of us. Victor was taking charge of his dream, and I was getting paid to read.

More and more my job was becoming something closer to that of a personal and professional assistant who occasionally put a meal on the table. I wasn't doing a lot of cooking since part of my boss's search for himself involved exploring life as a noncelebrity. He'd become fascinated by where the average man ate, so I picked up takeout everywhere, from the Sizzler to Burger King. He was definitely off his diet and at times I feared out of his mind. I drew the line at sampling ninety-nine-cent tacos. That called for an intervention and I had no trouble boldly stepping in. But most of the time I went along with his program and didn't take it personally that he wasn't craving my chicken piccata because I was too busy trying to think like a movie producer. I'd made notes on the book and a list of questions for discussion: Are these characters likeable? Where's the conflict? Can we write in a character for Julia Roberts? When I ran these questions by Victor, he said, "I didn't hire you to think like everyone else in Hollywood."

"Oh great," I said. "Now I've got to figure out how everyone in Hollywood thinks and think differently. I deserve to be paid overtime."

He just laughed and helped himself to another Burger King fry. My boss may have been in a jovial mood but he'd turned into a taskmaster. I can't complain, though, because by the time I finished my new assignment, I'd come up with a set of script notes that were solid yet breezy and even a little seductive, not unlike my best chocolate soufflé.

aniel's company was housed on the studio lot. The office was large and intimidating. There was expensive art on the walls, modern minimalist decor and, most intimidating of all, Daniel's smile—a smile that, if you didn't know better, could allay your fears because it seemed so warm and welcoming, but if you knew his reputation, you feared the smile. It was too inviting, too charming and too deceiving. The word on Daniel was that he liked to hug people because that made it easier for him to stab them in the back. No question about it, the guy was tricky. The thing is, he was such a good hugger and an even better talker. Even though you knew it was bullshit when he actually got into his spiel about how lucky you were that you weren't him, you ended up genuinely commiserating. When he rattled off the headaches he had on the job, you temporarily forgot he was doing it to discourage you from feeling envious. Envy created resistance and Daniel was a genius at getting friends and foes to disarm while he kept a knife in his pocket. Power was his big weapon.

It wasn't only that he knew all the top people in the business, but he'd done favors for all of them, which meant they all owed him. He also had strong connections to the media. Journalists from *The Wall Street Journal, The New York Times,* and the L.A. *Times* had been in his camp forever. They'd written flattering profiles of him in return for off-the-record insider info and gossip on stories about Daniel's foes. The result was that people in Hollywood feared him and people outside of Hollywood knew of him. He was one of the town's most famous off-camera players. Until I met Daniel I used to think that you could divide Hollywood into fame chasers and passionistas. But no one had more passion than he did—it was just that his passion was all about getting and staying famous.

Daniel did not keep us waiting long. Later Victor told me that in his experience the really smart powerful people in Hollywood tend to run their meetings on time. It's the mid-level executives or those people who have attained

their position by kissing the right ass who keep you hanging while they talk on the phone to their real estate agent.
Daniel was too smart to waste time—his or anybody else's.
He didn't even waste a second on any awkwardness over
the fact that he was now dating Claire. Then again, for a
guy like Daniel, Claire was a footnote, not something you
spent valuable meeting time discussing. Unless, of course,
she could be used in one of his master manipulations, and
I certainly wasn't savvy enough to figure that one out. All
I can say for sure is that Daniel acted as if Victor was not
only the most important person in the room, but possibly
the most important person on the lot. In Hollywood, flattery works. At least short term.

For twenty minutes Victor pleaded his case. He wanted
to buy Daniel and Claire out of their position on the project, or at least buy Claire out. His reasons were clear. He understood the material. The author of the novel was now on
his team. He would star in the film for a tenth of his usual
salary. He would use his clout to promote the film. All over
the world. He'd go to Cannes to pre-sell foreign rights. He'd
go to Siberia if that's what it'd take. He was articulate and
persuasive.

Daniel listened attentively. He'd halted all calls so we
wouldn't be disturbed. He didn't rush the pitch or interrupt.
But when Victor finally finished, Daniel took a second and
then said, "Why are you wasting your time with this?" And
then without waiting or wanting an answer, he launched
into his pitch for why Victor should abandon this project. It
mostly had to do with "this stage" of Victor's career and
how he needed to be working with directors and material

that were a good fit for him. Daniel talked a lot about Victor's audience and what they wanted to see from him at "this stage." He also flattered Victor but it was flattery meant to make Daniel feel good about himself. He wanted to feel like a good guy even though he was slamming the door on Victor's big dream. Happens all the time in Hollywood. Daniel didn't become mega successful by playing a selfless Santa Claus, and he was under no obligation to do a favor for an old friend. What bothered me was all that talk about what was good for Victor's career. It was very possible that if Victor pulled this off it would be very, very good for his career. What Daniel was really saying was that to be in business with an action hero on his way down wasn't good for his own career. The fact that Victor discovered the book in the first place was inconsequential. Books were real estate in Hollywood. Doesn't matter that you found the house, all that mattered was who got into escrow first.

When Daniel finished flattering Victor, he turned to me. "What do you think of this book?" Before I could answer, he added, "Didn't you used to be a chef?"

That question tells you a lot about Daniel. He seems to have the info on everyone. I almost blurted out, Christ, do you have dossiers on all of us? But it wasn't my meeting so I wasn't free to blow it.

"I still am. It keeps me in touch with my nurturing side. I don't want to turn into a guy." A shorter answer might have been more appropriate but Daniel's smile told me he appreciated the thought, though he lost no time getting back to the point.

"So what do you like about this book?"

I was ready for the question and had in fact rehearsed

an answer. "It's like a guidebook. It's a how-to-be-happy story for people who aren't lazy."

He tapped his fingers on his very expensive Frank Lloyd Wright desk. "Here's the problem with that. We make movies for lazy people. We make movies for people who are tired of their job and their life and don't want to have to figure anything out. We give it to them fast and easy because that's all they can handle and all that they want." He looked over to Victor. "Right, Mr. Famous?"

Dropping my nickname for Victor didn't surprise me. I wouldn't have been shocked if Daniel referred to our blood types. The guy had some information network.

"That is what *you* do," Victor agreed.

"And what made you a movie star." Daniel was up and walking around, like a professor who was confident he was the smartest guy in the room. "Which is why there's a problem with *Last Standing*. We bought the script because it is a simple summer action film. Your director is fucking it up by trying to get too clever. Your character is in Special Forces but he hates violence? Get the Gandhi shit out of the picture. I told Shane that if he wants to do that kind of movie, go make it for Harvey. Go work for Miramax. And what's with the art direction? There's no color on the screen. What's with all the gray in every shot?"

I braced myself. If he was going to attack Shane, I was going to have to breach the etiquette of a studio meeting and not only speak out of turn but vociferously defend my (so far) one-time lover. I don't let anyone trash someone I've fucked. Good sex makes me fiercely protective. That's when I turn into a kick-ass action character. But Daniel moved on, following up his attack on Victor's most recent movie with a little self-deprecation. "I'm going to get out of this business. No one listens to me. Maybe I don't know anything."

It was a nice attempt at some kind of ego balance, but even I knew the only reason he could say such a thing was because he was sure he knew everything and people clamored for his advice. Daniel's bogus self-deprecation was the equivalent of a supermodel saying she didn't think of herself as pretty. Still, it was hard not to give Daniel credit. Here was a guy who had started life on maybe the fifty-yard line and had made it all the way. Touchdown. However, as I watched Daniel strut around his fiefdom, I wondered if covering fewer yards but doing it with athletic grace and no dirty plays was more impressive.

"Daniel," Victor said when there was an opportunity to break into the monologue. "Just say it. Just go on record as saying no. Let's keep it simple. I'm asking you to work with me on *Skate* and you're voting no. So just say it."

Daniel sat on the edge of the desk, backlit by the window that overlooked the curved driveway where his car and driver were waiting to take him to his lunch at The Grill. "What else have I been saying for the last fifteen minutes?"

"You've been saying a lot of things and I know what it means but I just want you to say it. Say no."

"You want me to say no even though I've already said it."

"I want you to say that word, that one syllable that isn't about hedging bets or explanations or anything else."

Daniel was not amused. He didn't like abiding by someone else's rules.

"Is there some reason you need to hear that word?"

"Yes."

"Can you explain it in thirty seconds?"

Victor wasn't insulted by the time limit. Calmly he continued. "Because clarity is a beautiful thing."

"What haven't I been clear about? No, don't answer that. Forget it. I don't have time." Daniel glanced out his window to make sure his car was ready. "I wish you the best with this," he said, and hugged Victor goodbye.

Riding down in the elevator I couldn't help myself. I had to ask. "Clarity is a beautiful thing? Where did that come from?"

"Earl." He smiled.

"Ah," I said, as if it explained everything. I put it in the same mental box with Victor's fascination with increments, his interest in moving vans and his newfound love for Burger King fries.

As we reached the ground floor, he held the door open for me. "Notice Daniel never did say it. He never said no."

"I noticed," I said. "I don't get why you wanted him to say it but I did notice he didn't."

"Because people in Hollywood avoid the definite no just in case the issue comes around again and circumstances change. They prefer to pass on ideas and projects. They put things in turnaround. They move on. They revisit, revise and reconsider. The language says it all. We're living in a culture that wants to keep things so fluid, accountability and taste are never an issue. I say bring back the definitive, emphatic no, which would bring back the definitive, emphatic yes."

It may not have been the sanest of arguments but I

think I understood what he meant. In fact as Daniel's Town Car pulled out of the studio, it occurred to me that the great legends in Hollywood—both on and off the screen—are the type that have no trouble with a definitive yes or a definitive no. For a moment, I got nostalgic for that time when passionistas and fame chasers didn't come in the same package.

thirty

O n my return from Vegas, I called Shane and learned that he was out of town. The message on his voice mail said he'd be gone for three weeks. He might as well have said forever. People drift away from each other in three days in Hollywood. I knew one couple who got together on a Friday. On Saturday, he left for London for a month. By the time he got back she'd gotten married, gotten an annulment and was engaged to a new guy. True story. That's what can happen in a month.

Maybe it was better. I needed to get my life together before I could embark on the kind of chaos that comes with a new fling. I needed to stop living out of boxes and the trunk of my car. I needed solitude. I needed my own bed. It was essential that I reintroduce myself to the concept of "home." Being displaced is a logistical nightmare. Mail gets lost. Calls get lost. You lose track of what's at the dry cleaners. Your internal navigating system gets blown to smithereens. I felt physically safe staying up at Victor's, but in peril of losing my mind.

My equilibrium was not helped by an erotic dream. It was disconcerting to wake up after having such a vivid realistic dream about fucking my boss that I would not have been surprised to see him lying next to me in bed. It's not as if I'd had any fantasies that might have prepared me for what happened in that dream. Since no one really wants to hear the play-by-play of someone else's fantasy sex life, I'll skip the details and just say it was as if his dick came with its own built-in sonar device. No one found my G-spot faster or visited longer.

Making breakfast the next morning with him sitting at the kitchen table was a new experience. Suddenly I was self-conscious the way girls sometimes get after they've reached intense levels of physical intimacy with a new love, and the way I always get given my fear of emotional vulnerability. Even though Victor had been in some kind of hyper-motivated but self-isolation mode, spending hours every day on his computer (I prayed he wasn't writing a screenplay like everyone else who hits a career slump in Hollywood), he picked up on my seismic shift. Not that the symptoms were subtle.

"What's this?" He was holding up his fork with a piece of scrambled egg on it. A fairly large chunk of egg, which stuck on his fork easily. Of course it would because I'd overcooked it to the point where it appeared to be a slice of frozen cheddar.

"I'm sorry. I'll make you some more." I reached for his plate. He blocked my attempt. "What's going on?"

"Nothing." What could I say? That I couldn't stop myself from thinking about what was under the Adidas sweats he was wearing.

"You sure?"

His hand was still on my wrist, which made me blush, so I said the one thing that always gets a guy to back off fast.

"It's nothing. Just a girly medical thing."

He released his grip, as if PMS were contagious. I walked back over to the kitchen counter and started cracking a couple of eggs and contemplating my next move.

partment hunting in Los Angels is a nightmare. Real estate agents are useless. They're not interested in apartment rentals because their commission is so small. I don't blame them except when they act like they know exactly what you're looking for and can find you something perfect and then fax over a list of dumps. After looking at one particularly seedy place—asking price $2,200 a month—in a building managed by an old man who wore a tattered plum velvet robe and had at least four smelly cats, I asked my realtor if he'd even looked at the place before recommending it. Of course he hadn't. He'd just pulled it up off the listings.

Driving around looking for buildings with FOR LEASE signs is not much better. Even if the building looks decent from the street, chances are the available apartment is in the back, with windows that only afford a view of an alleyway and maybe, seeing as this is California, a little greenery thriving between cement walls. You also have to contend with calling the number on the FOR LEASE sign and getting a recorded message, which is actually about a rental down the street in a building you have no interest in. Or you leave a message and never hear back. Meanwhile your cell phone bill is climbing and your spirits are sinking.

I considered moving back into the house I'd been renting in my pre-stalker days. My stuff was still there. The lease had another three months on it. But when I drove over to check it out, there was one long-stemmed rose left outside the front door. The head of the flower had been torn off its stem. I got back in my car in a hurry and resumed my search for sanctuary everywhere from Silver Lake to Venice Beach.

I was beginning to understand Victor's interest in moving vans. Moving shakes things up. Even if you're moving to a bigger, better place (which I wasn't), there are still numerous, possibly unpleasant, unknown factors. Will the new roof leak? Are you on a canyon road that turns into mud in the rainy season? Did you move next door to someone with really bad taste in music and outdoor speakers? Does a neighbor down the block throw late parties? Or if in an apartment, does the woman upstairs come home at two A.M. and stomp around in her stiletto heels on hardwood floors? Does the couple on the other side of your bedroom wall have loud sex? The more I considered these issues, the more aware I became of the unavoidable anxieties that come with any transition. I began to understand that watching a moving van load up was watching people in the act of venturing into the unknown. No wonder Victor was fascinated.

He continued to spend most of his time in his office, which gave me a lot of time to escape from the stress of not finding a home. I read the entire collection of Ross Macdonald mystery novels. Lew Archer's adventures on the shady side of sunny So-Cal made me realize that women do not make good detectives. Their intuition might be superior to men's but you've got to throw vanity out the window to really do the rough-and-tumble work of a P.I., and I have yet to meet one woman in L.A. capable of that. I wasn't even capable of thinking about my own stalker. I had to live in at least quasi-denial or I'd get a rash on my left hand and on a strip of skin near my right ear. Stress-related skin disorders can be harder to figure out than any crime plot. So I did my best to stay distracted, which was why when Victor walked into the kitchen with a stack of printed-out notes and a new job for me, I was ready to say yes before he'd even explained the mission.

"How much do you think it would cost to rent out the downstairs at the Chateau?"

"Are you planning a party?"

"Better."

Action-hero actors sometimes branch out into directing, writing and producing. Some even contemplate a career in politics. Some even win the election. But Victor was the first, to my knowledge, to take up teaching.

Once a week, he took over the large elegant downstairs room at the Chateau Marmont. It was a site that was often used for book and promotional parties, usually when a corporation was footing the bill. It wasn't cheap, especially when you added in the cost of hiring parking valets. The Chateau might have loads of charm and Hollywood history but virtually no real estate when it came to garage space.

The plan was to hold open seminars—free of charge—

to talk about movies. Victor would share his knowledge and experience with young people trying to break into the business. This was not another Learning Annex class where some mediocre filmmaker inflates his own ego in front of a room filled with naive students who have to pay to hear the speaker laud himself. Victor would give useful information. Everything from why you should never let the makeup department talk you into getting tanning treatments—your skin will smell for a week—to why doing too many TV interviews detracts from the mystique of an action hero.

He would also give detailed tips on how to deal with very specific people in the industry. Casting directors, producers, agents, etc. DETAILED. He knew which ones loved to be flattered and which ones would only respond to you if you acted like you didn't care whether or not you got the part. He knew which ones told it to you straight and which ones would string you along over three callbacks and then cast their girlfriend—or boyfriend. It would be the kind of conversation a Hollywood insider might have over a lunch at The Grill with another insider. It was not what a star was supposed to share with a room full of strangers.

No one who worked for Victor thought this was a good idea. Not his agent, or manager, publicist or lawyer. Not that he was taking their calls. And if he did, they wouldn't understand that this was his way of trying his luck at another casino. I loved the idea but I was skeptical about it working. How would Victor promote it? Radio ads? A notice in the trades? Who would show up? It's not like he was offering free booze. He had none of these concerns. He simply called up his buddy Pat O'Brien at "Access Hollywood," and the next night in between stories about George

Clooney's new movie and Colin Farrell's new girlfriend was a twenty-second item on what soon came to be known as Hollywood University.

The crowd, which increased each week, was energetic and attentive and appreciated Victor's candor when it came to his ulterior motive. He told them outright, "Look, I did this film *Last Standing*, which the studio hates, and I'd love your help in figuring out where I went wrong. Or maybe I didn't go wrong. Maybe the studio's wrong. You tell me." He'd gotten a print of the film and against studio policy showed it in one of his classes. The students loved having input. Sometimes I'd stand in the back of the room watching all these intelligent young minds match up against Victor's experience and his newly developed curiosity and I'd think, He just might be operating on a whole other level. He wasn't trying to win any arguments, possibly because he understood that the dialogue itself made him a winner. Whether it was a belief in karma or knowing the law of physics that guarantees that energy is never lost, Victor conducted these classes with the calmness of someone who trusted that somewhere down the line, this would have an impact. Even if it would take a decade before one of these kids was in the position to call "Action."

And so the word spread. I don't think Bruce Willis could have gotten more buzz. A month in, the place was packed and the weekly tab for the parking valets was astronomical. My job was to make everything go smoothly, which took more prep time than you might imagine. It cut into my apartment hunting, which was okay because I hadn't had another erotic dream, so staying up at Victor's was still manageable.

Once the seminar was actually in session, I often slipped out to grab a coffee and do a few errands. One day as I was drinking a cup of Starbucks and checking out the magazines at a newsstand on Sunset, I came across an item on Layla in *US Weekly*. She must have been bummed that they never ran anything on her triangle "sisuation" in Vegas, but they gave prime coverage to a shot of her on the ground outside a Miami nightclub. Apparently she'd tripped and fallen after a long night of partying. It was the kind of pic that would probably inspire Layla's publicist to do damage control by planting stories about Layla's newfound (nonexistent) sobriety.

If I were a bitch I would have bought the magazine and showed the photo to Victor. But thoughts about my own bad karma made me put *US Weekly* back on the rack and go for that day's *New York Post*. I went right for the sports coverage, which is when it happened.

"Told you the Lakers were over."

I immediately closed the *Post*, as if not reading Pete Vecsey's commentary on the western finals would make the voice go away.

"Told you," Matt repeated.

My stalker was now standing right in front of me.

"Did you?" I replied. "I'm not really following the play-offs."

Sports talk had been off-limits with Matt for a while. Ever since the Super Bowl of 2002, when he chastised me for picking the Patriots. "Why is it that girls always pick the underdogs? When are you going to get that you go for the team that's the strongest? You go for the Alpha team. You go for the side that has the ammunition."

At the time I was tempted to say this country was founded by underdogs who were not considered the "Alpha team" and certainly didn't have the best ammunition, but pointing this out would only prolong a conversation I didn't want to have in the first place. I remember he lectured me for ten minutes about my stupid choice and then of course was stone cold silent when the Patriots staged an upset win.

"It would have been nice to get the four-peat," he said, "but maybe it's a good thing to give another team a chance for a ring."

Who is this guy? I thought. He looks like Matt, but Matt was never exactly a live-and-let-live kind of guy. He had some good qualities but generosity of spirit toward opposing teams was never one of them. Plus, he had a copy of *The New Yorker* in his hand—which was as jarring as if a wild frat boy at a sports bar was perusing a copy of *Martha Stewart Living* while a heavyweight bout was airing on the restaurant's wide-screen TV.

"Yeah," I said because I didn't know what else to say.

"Things good with you?" he asked.

"Not bad."

"You look good."

"Do I? Thanks."

"I thought about you the other day because I was at Dan Tana's and I have to say your pasta bolognese is better."

"Oh, well, that's sweet of you to say but I don't think so." I anxiously checked out the approaching traffic as if waiting for a bus . . . or a cop.

And that's the way it went for another five minutes.

He was perfectly nice, flattering, soft-spoken—and even kind . . . and it terrified me. It forced me to consider the possibility that maybe Matt wasn't my stalker. And if he wasn't—who was?

This new possibility rattled me so much that I bumped into a woman in the lobby of the Chateau and then while apologizing spilled coffee all over her Converse sneakers. A laugh from behind caused me to swing around and find Elizabeth West standing there.

"Meet my klutzy friend Lucinda," she said, addressing the woman I'd collided with. Elizabeth held my Starbucks cup as I wiped my coffee-splattered hands on my jeans and managed a hello to her friend, whose name was Kristen Spillers.

"Wow, your name is Spillers and I just spilled my coffee all over you. How weird is that?"

"Not weird enough," she said with a laugh.

Elizabeth explained. "Kristen works in publishing. She did an amazing job getting my book out there." Teasingly, she added, "We broke records in Temple City."

"My hometown," Kristen added. "Home of the San Gabriel Valley's Bridal District."

"Wow. A bridal district? Now that's weird." It was weird, but weirder was the fact that I kept saying "wow." I guess running into Matt was the equivalent of a minor concussion. My speech was slow, my vocabulary limited and clearly my motor skills were off. But no one seemed to notice. Not even Elizabeth, who praised her sales rep for getting her book prime placement in lots of stores. "And I'm not an easy sell," Elizabeth laughed. "My thank-you to her is a tour of the hot spots on Sunset. I promised her something even weirder than E!'s 'Celebrities Uncensored.' "

"Wow, that's great."

"What are you doing here?" Elizabeth asked.

"That," I said, pointing across the hallway to Victor's "classroom."

Kristen had already wandered over and was standing in the doorway. She waved us over. "Check this out."

Just then, Victor could be heard making a point, using the same commanding voice he'd displayed in one of his first films, *Jury's Out*.

"Where have I been? When did Mr. F turn into a lecturer?" Elizabeth asked.

"It's a long, long story," I said.

"Give me the one-liner."

"Action actor crashes but manages not to burn."

"Got it."

We stood in the doorway and watched Victor wrap up his show. He had the attention of everyone in that standing-room-only audience. He was talking about how it took him all these years to realize that what makes acting important is finding the truth in a scene, in a character. Finding it on the page is one thing and that's where it begins. But finding it in your soul is what it's all about. Otherwise you're just getting paid to lie, and the money is great but the lies take their toll. And there's always going to be someone who's a better liar, maybe simply because he hasn't been doing it as long so the audience hasn't caught on yet. "I've done enough steroids and lying in my career and let me tell you, after a while, it's fucking boring." He then concluded with an anecdote about why his favorite costar was a computer-generated alligator. And then as if this were a rock concert and the audience insisted on an encore, he finished up with a hilarious self-deprecating story about sharing an elevator in New York with Pamela Anderson and Alan Greenspan.

Watching and listening to him, my adrenaline started racing. Not unlike the way it had a half hour earlier when I'd walked away from Matt, full of fear and trepidation. Except it wasn't fear I was feeling now, it was excitement. Something was changing. Could be those increments were adding up and whatever they were adding up to, I knew I wanted to be a part of. WOW.

thirty-one

She wanted to get into it. Right then. Even if that meant talking till sunrise. She wanted to know where their relationship was going, a question that Mr. F had been asked by countless women over the last two decades, and he'd never come up with an answer that made any of them happy.

"I don't know where it's going but I'm going to bed."

"When will you know?" Claire hated herself for needing to know and hated him for putting her in a position where she ended up sounding like a bimbo grifter trying to close the deal.

He took a bottle of Evian out of the tiny refrigerator he'd had built into his walk-in closet. He twisted open the cap and took a swig.

Making her wait for a reply enraged Claire. It was always that way. Everything was on his schedule. How many times had she waited for him? To get off the phone. To sign an autograph. To finish another set of bench presses. To consult with his trainer. To talk to his chef. Always, always, waiting.

Before he could twist the cap back on the bottle, she'd taken off one of her spiked-heel Manolos and threw it at him. It missed his head by six inches but knocked over her half-filled glass that had been sitting on top of the bureau. Red wine spilled onto Mr. F's expensive beige Aubusson rug.

Claire was horrified by what she'd done. Sloppy was not her style but she couldn't bring herself to say I'm sorry. Too bad, because that was all it would have taken for Mr. F to let it go. But she said nothing. So neither did he. He silently grabbed her by an elbow, showed her to the door of the master bedroom and then shut it and locked her out.

"Fuck you, asshole." She pounded the door with her fist and her other shoe.

Calmly, he popped a CD into his new sound system, choosing the track from his last hit movie, 1999's summer blockbuster *Dare*. The louder Claire banged on the door, the louder he upped the volume. It was a contest she couldn't win and after a few minutes she gave up. A few minutes after that, Mr. F shut off the CD and turned on the TV. He assumed Claire would sleep in one of the guest rooms and tomorrow morning they'd deal with it—or not. He might have to take a break from this relationship but at that moment he was too tired to worry about it. He was also too preoccupied wondering if pouring Evian on a red wine stain would help or hurt the rug. Or was club soda a better choice?

He was almost asleep when Claire's other Manolo hit his window but didn't break through the safety glass.

"Fuck," she screamed and then laughed. A boozy laugh

that told Mr. F she'd spent the last hour or so having her own private cocktail party.

He went over to the window and saw that she was stumbling around his yard, wearing one of his sports coats over her dress and looking around the ground for something.

"Why don't you have any fucking rocks out here? Why is everything so, so . . . *manicured*?" She shrieked with joy as if finding that word meant she bested him in a duel.

Mr. F decided the smart thing to do was to call Gus up at the gatehouse. Gus was paid to handle incidents like this and paid even more to keep quiet about it, and Mr. F could see that Claire was too whacked to go away quietly. He walked away from the window over to the phone.

"Where did you go?" Claire screamed.

He had the receiver in his hand.

"Where the fuck did you go?"

He punched in the first number.

"You can't just walk away whenever you feel like it."

He heard Gus's phone ringing on the other end.

"Fuck you," Claire screamed again, only this time she followed up her words with a gunshot.

thirty-two

Everyone was there. Victor decided that with the studio's decision to just throw *Last Standing* out there with a minimal ad campaign and the unspoken message that they were writing it off, he would host his own screening on the lot. The studio agreed to let him use their largest theater, only if he agreed to schedule it on a Saturday afternoon and cover all expenses.

He'd brought his old assistant back into action on a full-time schedule to coordinate it and work on other things that were being done in a very hush-hush fashion. My only assignment was in the area of food. For a two P.M. Saturday screening that really came down to popcorn. I called around and found a company that made the best, healthiest popcorn in L.A. The guy on the phone claimed it was "even better than Newman's Own Oldstyle Picture Show Microwave Popcorn." That taken care of, I ordered the usual drinks—bottles of Evian and sodas, plus the entire selection of Glaceau Vitamin Water to suit every mood. Need to de-stress? Boost your energy? Calm down? There'd be a fruit-flavored water to help you through.

I wasn't worried about that part of the event, but I was anxious about seeing Shane again. Word was he was back in town and would be attending. I hadn't heard from him since that one message he'd left when I was in Vegas. I couldn't figure out if it was going to be awkward to see him again or wonderful.

But even wonderful couldn't compete with the carnival atmosphere that I experienced the second I drove onto the lot. Seems that Victor conjured up an event, not just a screening. The parking area was already crowded and people were in holiday spirits, as if on their way to fireworks on the Fourth of July. This was not your usual cynical industry crowd. The electricity in the air was crackling. A lot of the people getting out of those VWs and Wrangler Jeeps were regulars at Victor's seminars. And my boss was right there, up front and center, standing outside the theater welcoming his audience like a ringmaster outside his big top.

I ran into everyone I'd ever served dinner to since working for Victor. His best friend Lawrence was there with his new girlfriend, who I swear was indistinguishable from his last one. I even greeted her with a big friendly "Hi there, Rikki. How are you doing?"

"I'm Cassie," she said with petulance.

"Uh, sorry."

I was happy to exit that uncomfortable moment, even if it was to find myself face-to-face with Isabel, Victor's ex-wife, who was walking around as if she'd just come out of a yoga class. Good posture can be really annoying. Who can walk around that erect when the world is so fucking hard to deal with? Maybe someone who has always had men paying her bills and thinks the phrase "Get real" means not blow-drying her hair.

She'd brought Lauren, whose new style of dressing I decided to take the credit or blame for. She was looking very much like the girl in that Guess ad I'd brought to her attention. Same low-rise lace-up jeans, a tiny top and jacket. Same chunky turquoise jewelry. Same everything except no hunky guy draped all over her. Give her another year, I thought. Lauren's friend Ceci was with her, sporting a new look, too. Her fascination with J.Lo was history and her new image (long, straight, in-her-face hair) seemed inspired by Avril Lavigne.

I roamed around, my eye out for Shane. Instead I bumped into Alex, Victor's agent, or ex-agent. Or was he?

"Haven't seen you in awhile," I said.

"That's true," Alex replied, not giving much away. "Who put together this focus group?" He was looking around the crowd at all the students.

"No one. These are all Victor's friends."

"Good, good," he replied.

An agent should know whether his client's screening involved a focus group or not, which suggested that Alex was out of the loop. But in or out, he didn't look worried. He was the ultimate in that other kind of cool—not the kind that required the right accessories, but the kind that never panicked in clutch situations. Which, when you get right down to it, might be the only cool that really matters.

Of course, all of Victor's ex-girlfriends were there.

Stephanie, the notorious blow job girl, was wandering around. This time she was a little more friendly, probably because she was solo and needed someone to latch onto.

"Love this popcorn," she said.

"Gotta have popcorn."

"Gotta have a cigarette. Got one?"

"Nope."

"I guess I'll live." She put another popcorn kernel in her mouth.

Even the way she ate was sexual. It was the first time I'd seen her in daylight and I have to say that even though I knew she was around thirty-five, she looked like she was in her late twenties. More impressive was that there was no sign of aging around her mouth, which led me to wonder if maybe blow jobs were an age-defying exercise. However, the biggest surprise about this turnout was the appearance of Dr. Davenport. What did this mean? Had Victor continued sessions with the doc in spite of his cynicism? I had to find out.

"This is a shock," I said.

"I don't usually come to these sorts of things," he replied.

"Is it weird socializing with patients?"

"The only patient here is you."

Me? Really? Oh. For a second I felt as if I were experiencing early dementia.

"Did I invite you?"

"Victor did."

"Are you guys friends?"

"We talk."

I think this meant Victor managed to get one of the smartest guys in town to give him free advice. I wondered what was in it for Davenport, then a ten-year-old boy came up and pulled on the doc's arm.

"Hey Daddy, I saved you a seat."

I guess even a no-bullshit, brilliant shrink will drop his standards a little to get his son in on some Hollywood action.

It wasn't until I was inside the theater, looking for a seat, that I spotted Layla, who had brought a guy with her. Not Jonas, but a version of him. Leather jacket, scruffy T-shirt, jeans and, on his feet, three-hundred-dollar Pumas. I waved but she turned away. Snubbed by my dancing partner. Gee, if only I cared enough to miss a beat. I watched as her scruffy companion stepped back and gave her room to embrace Victor. The guy looked a little uncomfortable watching the girl he came with practically hump Victor's leg. Victor, on the other hand, politely and skillfully disentangled himself and then shook the guy's hand. I don't think it was the triangle situation that Layla was hoping for.

When the lights went down, two people slipped in and took their reserved seats in the back row. Daniel and Claire. I knew Daniel wasn't on the guest list, but his company financed the film so no one was going to keep him out of whatever screening he wanted to attend. I'm sure Claire loved being with the head honcho, and watching her acknowledge a few of Daniel's minions as if she were seated at the right hand of God made me momentarily ill. When she caught me watching, she threw me completely off guard by blowing me a kiss. I smiled back, but I didn't take her friendliness personally. I was just someone who worked for the guy that I suspected she was still in love with. She kept glancing across the aisle to the row where Victor was sitting but never caught his eye. Either he didn't know she was there or, I hoped, didn't care. As I watched the film, one mystery was solved. So this is what Victor was up to when he was clocking in all the private hours in front of his computer. Ah, the beauty of e-mail, downloading, attachments, digital copying and all the Internet services that make it possible for an actor in L.A. and his director in London to hatch a mini-conspiracy.

*L*ast *Standing* was initially meant to be a hard-driving action flick, clocking in at ninety minutes, no more, no less. I'd seen the studio's preferred version that Victor had run for his class, but this was my first look at the director's cut. Shane and Victor had conspired to ignore the studio notes and go back to their original inspiration. If Robert Kaye, the executive in charge of the project, was somewhere in the audience, it was very possible he was on his cell with an attorney for the studio the second the opening credits faded from the screen. Victor better enjoy this, I thought, because the big bosses are going to repossess this print, lock it up, throw their own version out in the marketplace and never work with Victor again.

The film up on the screen broke the rules of a summer action flick. It had character development. The stupid jokes were edited out. There wasn't a lot of bright colors in it, except in one shot, which was meant as a private p.s. (or fuck you) to Daniel, who'd complained about the muted tones. Now a meeting scene in a very gray warehouse included a digitally doctored bright red table. The movie worked for me but my opinion didn't count. It's not like I was "Cubicle Guy."

Cubicle Guy is a concept that Elizabeth West came up with. You can have a big success in Hollywood if your movie is a big-ticket event and the marketing campaign has practically brainwashed the population into showing up opening weekend. Doesn't hurt, of course, to suck up to well-known journalists, critics and magazine editors. That, however, does not mean your movie will have an impact. To accomplish that you've got to reach the guy in the cubicle—that person essentially is a factory worker at one of these big media outlets. His desk is probably in some tiny closet space not even close to a window. He has no expense account and no perks. He isn't connected to Hollywood or anyone who made the movie. He's just a guy with a computer in a cubicle assigned to write the small pieces. But if that guy, who isn't being paid to like your movie, writes about it out of genuine passion and with intelligence and keeps a buzz going through word of mouth and chat rooms, then you're on the road to making an impact. I reached into my pocket where I had a tiny pink crystal that had been given to me by the first chef I'd ever worked for. It was my good luck charm and I held it for a moment and said a silent prayer that somehow this version of the movie would have its day and that there was a Cubicle Guy somewhere in that audience.

The first person I saw when I stepped outside was Alex.

"The kids loved it," he said.

"Victor loves it," I said, looking over to where my boss was standing, surrounded by a half dozen of his students.

He was taking his time to respond to the person tapping him on the shoulder, a stern-looking portly man who clearly wasn't used to being kept waiting.

"Who's that?"

"Robert Kaye," Alex replied.

"Wow." I was genuinely shocked. That was Robert Kaye? The executive who had been torturing Shane and Victor through the whole shoot? He wasn't what I expected. "He's an import, isn't he?"

My conclusion was based on his dress and manner. Very Euro. He looked like he'd be right at home at some banker's meeting in Munich. It was rare for a Hollywood player to be an outsider. Whether a studio executive was artist friendly or corporate friendly, almost all of them had a familiarity about them. It was easy to imagine growing up next door to them on Long Island or in Encino. They were all quintessentially American.

"Eighteen months on the job," Alex said as he kept his eyes on Victor and Robert, who were now engaged in what looked like a heated conversation, with Robert doing most of the talking.

"Eighteen months. Clock's ticking," I said, and Alex smiled. He knew exactly what I meant. Hollywood was not a place for outsiders. Never has been. Never will be. Foreign investors were welcome but the day-to-day job of running the business could never be handled or even understood by someone who was not part of the community. Hollywood may look like an easy game to figure out, but the shifting power alliances in this town could only ever be deciphered by an insider. Even an outsider like myself knew that the imports are lucky to last two years.

"Clock's ticking," Alex repeated, laughing as he walked off in the direction of Victor and Robert, hopefully to bring some of his legendary cool to a potentially explosive situation.

I wandered around for another fifteen minutes looking for Shane but didn't spot him until I'd given up and was on my way back to the parking lot. He was heading over to an emergency meeting with Daniel.

"I was looking for you," he said. "Am I going to see you at the party?"

"What party?"

"Victor's."

"Victor's having a party? Where?"

"At his house. Now."

"What?"

Suddenly a familiar presence hovered nearby.

"Uh . . . Luce, does Orso do takeout for two hundred?"

thirty-three

The answer was no. We could not order two hundred, or even one hundred, pizzas from Orso. It was a real restaurant, not a Pizza Hut. But I did get them (as a favor) to sell us twenty-five of their famous thin-crust pizzas. Then I got on the phone to Koi, which also isn't a takeout establishment, to make up six large platters of sushi, which I had a messenger service pick up and deliver to the house. Finally, I put in an order at Koo Koo Roo for seventy-five original-recipe orders of chicken with sides of Caesar salad, cucumber salad and macaroni and cheese. A call to the Beverly Glen Market took care of the alcohol and beverages. Thank God for cell phones and credit cards. I accomplished all this in the distance it took to go from Washington Boulevard to the top of Motor and Pico. Problem was that now I was left with the rest of the drive back up to Victor's to worry about everything else, including the note I found in my glove compartment when I opened it to get the Evian water that I spritz on my face whenever I'm stressing out.

Lucinda, you can run but you can't . . . well, you know how it goes.

I frantically looked in my rearview mirror as if the author of the note might be tailing me, just like that scene in the movie *Duel*. It wasn't likely that the young woman in the silver Mini Cooper was my stalker. Nor the college-age kids behind her in their Ford convertible. I hit the accelerator anyway and sped back up to Victor's. Thank God for security gates, security guards and the Bel Air patrol.

The party was like no other that Victor had thrown at his house since I'd been in his employ. There were more people than he'd ever had over before and no celebrities, except for Sheryl Crow, who had recently bought a house nearby. Because it was last minute, there was no time to make up a list of guests, so Gus was instructed to take down the license plate number of every car that entered the enclave and the names of the driver and any passengers.

In certain cases he didn't stop there. Stephanie later laughed about how Gus was a big flirt, which she found harmless and funny because he flirted for the sake of flirting. He didn't expect a yes at the end of his corny come-on lines.

"Don't be so sure," I said. "I think he's one of those guys who doesn't mind that for every one girl who says 'maybe' he goes through nine hundred and ninety-nine rejections."

She thought about that for minute. "If that's true I have new respect for his tenacity."

"He's a guy. Tenacity is a given. They get tenacity, we get manipulation."

"I'd trade in a heartbeat," she said.

I thought about that for a minute. "Me too. As long as I could still keep stilettos, La Perla and YSL lipstick."

"Don't leave out blow jobs," she added.

I never saw Layla there. Guess she didn't make the cut. Or was she invited and decided to withhold as a strategy to get Victor's attention? I'm not sure he even noticed because the hush-hush business he had been up to over the past week had intensified. He and a half dozen of his students were in his office for about twenty minutes and they all came out in a good mood. At another time, another era, my guess would be drugs. But now I had to wonder what could possibly make them all so high. I figured I could ask Alex, but when I spotted him, he, along with a new group of students, was following Victor back inside.

Isabel was standing nearby but I doubt she'd know what was going on. However, right next to her were Lauren and Ceci. I bet on Lauren. She was a smart girl and had the daddy/daughter dynamic down to perfection. I'd once watched Victor try to reprimand her about something that had to do with school. "You can't do that, Lauren," he said, doing his best to be parental and set some rules. "It's not the way the world works. You can't go around acting like that." She listened to every word and then when he was finished, she said, "Daddy, I like that shirt on you." He adored her and she was the only one who could walk into that office without an invitation. I waited till Isabel was occupied at the buffet table before approaching Lauren and Ceci.

"Hi, girls."

"Hi," they said in unison.

"What's going on?"

"Just hanging out. Same old stuff."

No chance. Nothing was same old stuff when you're these girls at that age. "Where's your dad? I need to ask him a question."

"I think he's in his office."

"What's he doing there?"

"You don't know?"

"No."

I waited for her to tell me what it was but she had her mind on other things. "Oh my God. Is that Sheryl Crow?"

Feeling left out and alone, I helped myself to a vitamin water that claimed to boost one's determination, and reminded myself that I was Victor's chef. I wasn't his business partner or his girlfriend and maybe not even his friend. I considered him my friend but it's not like he'd ever introduced me as "my friend Lucinda." I'd always known it was dangerous for an employee to blur the line between professional and personal. Extremely dangerous. I had to take a step back, even though it was especially hard, now that I had a new note from my stalker in my glove compartment and more than ever could use an action hero, even a semi-retired one, on my team.

Finally, making his usual unpredictable entrance, Shane appeared seemingly out of nowhere. I'd been watching the cars drive in for the last hour but somehow had missed his arrival. He already had a bottle of beer in his hand and he sat down next to me.

"How was your meeting?" I said.

"Brutal."

"And yet you don't look worried."

"Guess I'm getting used to trouble."

He pulled a small wrapped package out of his jacket pocket and handed it to me. "I brought you something from London."

"How sweet. Should I open it now?"

"Sure."

Nervously, I tore off the paper to find a tube of sunblock SPF 40. I broke into a huge smile.

"So your butt doesn't get sunburned," he said.

"Is this your charming way of saying you'd like to do it again?"

"I wanted to be charming but couldn't come up with anything."

"But you did bring this all the way from London? That's pretty charming."

"Well, the duty-free shop."

"You do know I don't have a pool? I don't even have a home."

He grinned. "I have a pool."

I would have suggested exiting the party that minute but Victor had reemerged from the house and waved Shane over. I assumed it was just Shane he was calling, not the two of us, but Shane interpreted it as a plus-one situation.

"Let's check this out," he said.

"Check what out?"

"You don't know?"

"Know what?"

He took my hand. "Wait till you see this."

. . .

ictor sat at the desk in front of his computer, with Shane and I looking over his shoulder. It felt conspiratorial, which was part of the fun. Let Robert Kaye or Saint Daniel take over *Last Standing* and put it out the way they wanted. A three-minute promo of Shane and Victor's version of the film was NOW PLAYING on the Internet. Victor logged onto a site for film buffs and clicked onto the message boards. He cackled with great glee as he scrolled down to pages of enthusiastic responses to the *Last Standing*'s three-minute debut on the 'net.

"This is my favorite," he said. "It's from a guy in Des Moines. 'Shane Jackson deserves to die, if the rest of the movie is like that promo, that fuck made the film I've always wanted to make.' "

"What does this all mean?" I asked. I understood that somehow Shane and Victor got their tease for the movie on the Internet, which I'm sure was breaking a bunch of rules, or maybe even laws. But since the studio's cut was the one that would make it into the theaters, what good would it do?

Shane dropped his arm around my shoulder. "What it means, pine nut, is that we just threw a little tea into the Boston Harbor."

Victor beamed. Talk about how beautiful a face can look when it's filled with life. He *still* had the passion to fight the good fight *in spite of* working in a business that only has an ON/OFF button. Either you're hot or you're not. Wake up, Hollywood. There's a whole middle game about to fuck with your master plan. If I were going to fall in love with Victor it would have been at that moment, because it's hard not to swoon a little over a man who's got that much joy in him. I was reminded of that old Hollywood joke, dying is easy, comedy is hard. How about comedy is easy, joy (in this town) almost impossible.

n the mood for a swim?" I asked as Shane and I left Victor's office to make room for another group of guests who wanted their sneak peek. The sun was setting but I didn't think it'd be a problem to veer from our script. We didn't actually have to re-create our poolside passion. We could bring it indoors.

"Would love it, but I've got to be on a plane in an hour and a half."

"What? Where are you going?"

"Toronto. But I'll be back in a month."

"A month?" I thought of all the things that could happen in a month that would send us in different directions. He might as well have said a year. "Doesn't anybody stay in one place anymore?" I said, hoping that by casually tossing out a line from a Carole King classic, I might be able to disguise my disappointment. I was wrong.

"Cheer up," he said. "There's always e-mail."

thirty-four

As he ran down the stairs, Mr. Famous remembered that he'd once shown Claire where he kept his gun, in a box in the closet of his office.

"Why don't you keep it upstairs in case someone breaks in in the middle of the night?" she asked.

"Because no one will break in. This is a gated security-patrolled community." He never considered that the threat to his safety would come from an invited guest.

"So why have one at all?"

"It was a gift from the producer of *Arsenal*."

"Good movie," she said. She held the firearm in her hand. "Great gun."

When Mr. Famous got outside, Claire was sitting in the Porsche, no gun in sight. He would have preferred to keep track of the firepower because she was in no condition to exercise restraint.

"Get out of the car," he said.

"Get out, get in, get out, get in. Make up your fucking

mind. Not that it matters because I don't give a fuck what you want."

"I'll drive you home. Or stay here. Those are your choices."

"Yeah," she snarled. "Here are *your* choices. You can drive yourself somewhere and I'll . . . do something else."

He had never seen her this smashed before. He reached across her to grab the keys out of the ignition but they weren't there.

"Oh yeah, they fell on the floor somewhere."

He opened the passenger side and looked on the floor of the front seat.

"And then I found them." She laughed, holding up a key in her left hand. She exited on the driver's side, her shoulder bag firmly in tow, its bulkiness suggesting that that's where the gun might be. Tauntingly she said, "A little ammunition goes a long way."

She had no plan of action. Her only plan had been to have the last word. The gunshot had made the last word irrelevant. She'd had the loudest word. That was better than the last.

She savored her victory until a voice from her past—her mother's—reminded her it was rude to gloat. It's what her mother always said whenever she beat her siblings in a swimming contest. But her mother wasn't there and gloating was actually a lot of fun. Claire loved that she had really gotten to Mr. F at last. There he was, naked in the moonlight, unsure, not knowing if pursuing her was a good or bad idea. She turned to look at him, to bask in having the upper hand, when she saw that he was on the phone.

"Who are you calling?"

"The cops," he said, though he was lying. It was Gus on the other line. And Mr. F was furious. "A gunshot is fired and no one investigates? What the fuck kind of security guard are you?"

Claire did not want to include Gus or anyone else in her two-character melodrama. A neighbor across the road turned on the lights in front of his garage. "Spectators are not welcome," she yelled, though she hadn't meant to get quite so loud. A neighbor up the road yelled back, "Shut the fuck up."

She ran back to the car, but before she could get in, Mr. F grabbed her and held her arms by her sides.

"Let go of me."

"Throw your bag and the keys on the ground," he said.

"Let me go."

"Throw them down."

A car approached. Gus? Claire complied.

Mr. Famous let her go and the second he did, it struck her that he really was letting her go. This was it. He would never touch her again. She couldn't let it end like this. She needed to exit mad, not sad. Without thinking it through, she saw an opening and went for it. As he grabbed the stuff off the ground, she smashed her fist into his eye.

He never saw it coming. As drunk and volatile as she was, he never expected that. It wasn't the power of the punch that stunned him, it was the fact that the fighting instinct he prided himself on—both on and off the screen—had jammed. The proverbial slap in the face had momentarily paralyzed him.

Taking advantage of Mr. F's inertia, Claire jumped in the Hummer, knowing the gate clicker would be in there somewhere and she'd need that to get out of there. She lucked out—the keys were in the ignition and she had the car in gear before Gus could get out of his. If I have to crash through the front gate, I will, she thought, but a second later she located the clicker on the passenger-side visor.

As she turned onto the main road, she reached into the inside pocket of the sports jacket she had on, pulled out the gun and put it in the glove compartment.

For a minute she enjoyed her wild escape. I won. I won. I won. He's an asshole and I'm not going to take it anymore. It was a very short minute. In the contest for her state of mind, her sadness was making a strong comeback, forcing her to consider this question. If he was such an asshole, why was he the only thing she wanted to think about? I have to go back, she decided, and jerked the steering wheel hard to change direction, but the Hummer proved too much for Claire to handle.

thirty-five

Maybe June gloom is over, I thought on waking the next day. The overcast skies, which are typical for that time of year, had given way to early morning sunshine. Lunch on the patio seemed like a good idea, assuming Victor didn't have other plans. He did. "No cooking today," he announced. "We're raiding the refrigerator and having a feast of leftovers." We? Guess I was invited to join him.

We grabbed whatever looked good out of the fridge and carried it to the table outside the kitchen door. The conversation was light, casual. Normal. No work talk. No movie talk. No stalker talk. I decided there was no reason my problems should become Victor's problems. Inspired by the recovery he seemed to have made since that dark night last January, I was determined to find a place to live and get my life in better working order. As I reached for the classified section of the *Times*, I realized we had a guest.

"I want your life," Daniel said. He was standing in the

doorway as if it were his doorway. Daniel could do that. He could make wherever he was seem like it was his home even when it was yours. "I want to be able to sit around reading and hanging out on a beautiful day."

Victor smiled, as if having this studio honcho show up unannounced and intrude on his life without even ringing the doorbell was entertaining. "What'd you do, jump the fence?"

"My car's next door," Daniel replied. "I was looking at your neighbor's house, which is going on the market next week."

Leave it to Daniel to find access. It didn't matter that we all knew he wasn't doing any serious real estate shopping in the middle of the day. He had one of the best houses in town, just north of Sunset, west of Beverly Hills. We were never going to see a moving van outside that mansion.

"You and me, neighbors?" Victor smiled wryly. "That's a scary thought."

I cleared off some plates to make room for Daniel, in case he wanted to sit down, but he preferred to stand or occasionally pace.

"Hungry?" Victor asked him.

"No," he said, but picked up a piece of chicken and took a bite.

I went back into the house, closing the French doors behind me to give them some privacy, but Victor reopened them. Maybe he wants a witness, I thought. Maybe I'm supposed to record this for him. A stenographer without a notebook or pen. Or maybe I was just a Hollywood voyeur.

. . .

aniel pulled a thin contract out of his pocket, held it up and then with a flourish tore it in half and threw the pieces on the table. "Claire's option on *Skate* has expired."

Victor barely glanced at the torn agreement. "It was a year option; she's got till next February."

"It expired early," Daniel repeated, "and she walked away with a nice check. It's your book if you want it."

"Why?"

"Fuck why. Here's the deal. Two hundred thousand for a first draft. If we decide not to continue, you'll still own the option and the script."

"Why are you doing this, Daniel?"

"Because do you know how many messages were logged in on the Internet about *Last Standing*? From all over the country. I fucking hate the three-minute promo but I'm a forty-three-year-old man who's getting paid a lot of money to take an educated guess on what fifteen-year-olds want to pay ten bucks to see. So you and Shane do it your way but we control the sound track and ad campaign."

Victor didn't respond right away but I was loving the show. Even the heavy pauses. I loved watching Daniel reverse himself—not on the project as much as on Victor. He had been all set to write him off as a loser. An actor whose career was in decline. A guy who had shot his load. Daniel was almost never wrong about these things but now he realized that Victor might be on to something with *Last Standing*, and might even be on to something with *Skate*. Daniel wanted a piece of that and getting it required damage control. For Daniel that came down to trying to sound as honest as possible and putting enough on the table so that even if the honesty act didn't fly, he'd still have a shot at a deal.

"You're going to control the sound track and ad campaign? What does that mean? Crap songs and ads that make it look like we're putting out the same old shit?" Victor was enjoying himself and seemed unconcerned about the possibility of blowing the offer.

"Have Alex call me and we'll work it out," Daniel said. He went to leave and stopped abruptly. "One more thing, I have something for you."

In a minute he was back, carrying a framed photograph.

It was one of Claire's nude self-portraits from her gallery show. "You want this?" Daniel asked, handing it to Victor.

"I already have one," Victor replied. He looked confused and so was I. When Daniel came bearing gifts to actors he wanted to woo, it was usually something a little more "useful."

"We broke up," Daniel explained. "She says I screwed her on this *Skate* project. I told her she screwed you on the project, I'm just returning stolen property."

Daniel leaned the photograph against the wall. "What should I do with this? What did you do with yours? It's someone's artwork. Can't trash it. Can I?"

Translation: Daniel would trash his relationship with Claire, maybe with anyone, for the right deal. Looking at me for the first time since he arrived, he said, "Do you want this?"

"No, but I have an idea of someone who might."

"Who?"

I tuned to Victor. "Gus?"

He laughed. "Perfect."

• • •

For fifteen minutes Victor and I reveled in the rush that comes from getting something you want on your terms. It happens so rarely, and lasts so briefly, but it's great to be cruising at that altitude even if I was just along for the ride. It makes you want to spread the joy . . . and the news. Victor leaped up and said, "I've got to call Shane." When he went to his office to get his director's number in Toronto, I fantasized about the e-mail that I'd send later that night. It was probably the fiftieth time I'd mentally composed a message to Shane. Hadn't yet worked up the nerve to send any, but with June gloom gone, this could be the day.

The sound of footsteps quietly approaching didn't alarm me. I assumed it was Victor. On second thought, I realized my boss walked with a heavier step. Oh well, maybe Daniel forgot something. I looked over to the doorway and gasped.

"Hi, baby."

I couldn't speak.

"It's customary to say hi back. I don't expect a term of endearment but 'Hi Matt' would be nice."

I forced words out though I would have been more comfortable screaming. "Why are you here?"

He sat down at the table, edged his chair closer. "We run into each other at the newsstand, everything is fine, and you never call?"

"I run into a lot of people at newsstands that I don't call. What's there to say?" Wrong question. He might take that to mean this was his window of opportunity to list his grievances. "Forget that. How did you get inside the gate?"

"It was open."

It would only have been open if someone who lived here or an approved guest was driving in or out. It was possible Matt could have slipped in but not without Gus noticing, unless . . . Gus was too distracted because he was looking at a photo of Claire naked. A scenario that was so very possible, it was almost as scary as a surprise visit from my ex.

I picked up the phone to call the guardhouse but Matt took the mobile out of my hand.

"Wait," he said. "Don't get all paranoid and fucked up."

That's when I lost it. "What am I supposed to 'get' when you . . ." I ran down my list of everything he'd done over the last four months. He listened quietly and attentively. An observer would have thought he was the reasonable one and I was the lunatic.

When I ran out of accusations, he took over.

"For the sake of argument, let's say I did those things. What's wrong with complimenting you on the color of your dress? Noticing you need better locks on your windows? Have you never left a friendly note in someone's car? Got a little drunk and left a song in someone's voice mail?"

Seven messages, I corrected.

"Maybe your phone system was fucked up and kept cutting off my message, so I had to rerecord. Ever think about that?"

"Was the paint job on my car fucked up so you had to keep running your key over it?"

"Maybe that wasn't me. But maybe I was the guy who left a long-stemmed rose outside your door."

"With the head of the flower ripped off."

"Maybe it fell off. Ever think a neighbor's cat could have chewed it off?"

He picked up a knife that was on the table. His back was to the hallway and he didn't see Victor approaching. Nor did he hear him because Victor was wearing swimming trunks and was barefoot.

The surprise factor would be critical in taking control of the moment. I'd watched enough of Victor's movies to know that.

"Do you want me to make you lunch, Matt?" My voice was exceptionally loud and came out a little British. I was hoping that the look on my face and the name Matt would alert my boss that we had a situation here.

"Okay. I'll have lunch with you and your Mr. Famous."

"He's not around at the moment, *Matt*." I overdid the emphasis on Matt's name and thought for sure he knew what I was doing and would turn around to see Victor stopped a few yards from the doorway.

Instead, he looked at the two cups of coffee on the table. "Whose cup is this?"

"Someone from the studio dropped off some papers." The torn *Skate* contract was still on the table.

"Pre-shredded." He laughed.

I couldn't bring myself to join him.

"Don't you think that's funny?" He stood up and over me, the knife still in his hand. Using the tip of it, he tried to lift the corner of my mouth into a half smile.

That's when Victor made his move. Locating the exact pressure point and applying the right amount of force to Matt's sternum, he literally took Matt's breath away. A second later the knife was dropped. Except for the opponent and the location, it was precisely what Victor did when he played a commander in the 1993 film *Copter Eight*. Making an adjustment that allowed Matt to take in air, Victor continued to hold him with a viselike grip and spoke right into his ear.

"You got two choices. Either recognize the dead end that this is or I'll introduce your head to the brick wall you're about to crash into."

Ouch. Bad line. Victor was not the greatest ad-libber but so what? Those biceps of his were pumped up.

Matt nodded his head, because when he tried to speak Victor intensified the pressure on his ribs.

"No. Not a word. Not one word. Not to her. Not to me. Ever. Got it? We understand each other?"

Matt nodded again.

Victor let him go.

Matt fell to the floor and looked up imploringly. "Can I just say one thing?"

"No," Victor replied. "Okay. One."

Matt looked at me. "I didn't rip the top off the rose."

I didn't say anything but I kind of believed him.

He stood up.

Victor opened the door. "Okay, now get out of here."

"One more thing?" Matt asked. "The last thing?"

"The very last," Victor said.

"Can I have your autograph?"

thirty-six

Late afternoon in the summer is the best time to be up in the canyon. It was warm enough to go for a swim even if the pool wasn't heated, which of course it was.

Time for a new chapter. Step one—get out of the kitchen more often and not just for the occasional sex or shopping adventure. If I wanted to get moving off that fifty-yard line, I was going to have to learn how to fight my own version of the good fight. And enjoy it. In spite of that resolution, I did get a big charge out of my latest shopping purchase, a thank-you present for the boss. I'd had a T-shirt made up that said VICTOR FAMOUS, my way of saying I liked him and his persona.

When I got to the pool, Victor was there doing laps. It was the first time he'd dove in since January 12 and the Claire Neville incident. Before his crack-up, he swam every day as part of his maintenance program. His return to an activity that he loved was proof that a return to normalcy was underway. There'd been a few times, including the previous day, when he'd suit up, only to remain pool-side, in a lounge chair, to catch a few rays. Had Matt not shown up, maybe he would have taken the plunge twenty-four hours sooner, but that incident momentarily slowed him down.

"Oh, sorry. I'll come back later," I said, as I put my towel down on a lounge chair.

Victor pushed his wet hair off his face. "I think the pool is big enough for two people."

I felt like I was intruding but it was my last day living there so I went with it. I stepped into the shallow side and stayed there while Victor and I talked like we'd known each other a lifetime. He talked about his plans for *Skate*. He talked lovingly about his brother, about Earl, and his daughter. He told me funny stories and encouraged my fanciful ideas, and suddenly I had a mini epiphany that could become a major epiphany if I managed to hold on to it for longer than a summer afternoon.

I realized how grateful I was that Victor existed and that his spirit was alive and well. That's not the epiphany part. That came a second later when it hit me that even if I stopped working for him someday, because things changed and he didn't need a chef, and even if he drifted out of my life and we never saw each other again, it would be okay.

Drifting apart is part of living here. Hollywood is a place where things shift more rapidly than they do other places. People move on because the world we live in requires it. Our needs, even our identity, change more often here, and it's harder to know which side of the line things fall on. Was Claire a good person who had a crazy episode? Was Matt a crazy person who was capable of normal episodes? Was a fun night of dancing with Layla irrelevant because she and I barely say hello to each other anymore? Was Shane interested in me for a minute or would that minute turn into an hour? A day? A week? A year? Hard to say. With the confusion level high and the ground always shifting, survival calls for encouraging spirit wherever you find it—not trying to own it. And if that sounds too much like my (and maybe your) least favorite Sting song (If you love somebody, set them free, blah, blah, blah), then all I can say is I'm sorry for sounding so earnest and I won't let it happen again.

But the story doesn't end there. My swell of undeclared emotion was met with what I call an act of nondenominational goodness. An act at the core of all faith, hope and charity. A gesture worthy of an action hero.

"So, Luce, are you doing okay?"

"Yeah, I'm fine," I said.

And that's when he said it. It was a question so simple and yet so big that I made a mental note to ask my friends this very thing from time to time. It was a question that lets someone know they're not alone now—no matter how solitary they may feel. It was a question uttered, in one way or another, by all action heroes.

"How can I help you, Luce?"

And even though I didn't have an answer, I swam over toward Victor and into the deep end of the pool.

acknowledgments

A big thank-you to:

—Eric and Lisa Eisner for too many reasons to mention
—Peter Benedek for helping me keep the faith
—Stacey Sher, Susan Campos, Merle Ginsberg, Dana Garman, and Barbara Benedek for the great girltalk
—Stephen Hopkins for being such a great pal
—Chris Brancato and Bert Salke for their brilliant advice and fun lunches
—Julie Grau, Owen Laster and Alexandria Morris for being the perfect blend of savvy and sensitive
—Art Luna for his good-luck charm
—Louie Eisner for letting me steal the words off his painting for one of the book's best T-shirts
—Priscilla Woolworth and Kendall Conrad for all their encouragement
—Amanda Scheer Demme for making things happen
—And, as always, BIG THANKS to "Sidney the Great" for living up to his nickname

about the author

Carol Wolper is also the author of the novels *The Cigarette Girl* and *Secret Celebrity*. She lives in Los Angeles.